ONE HUNDRED CHOICES

AN ASPEN COVE SMALL TOWN ROMANCE

KELLY COLLINS

BOOK NOOK PRESS

CHAPTER ONE

A woman should never let a man take away her choices. That was Trinity Mosier's mantra. She'd told herself that a thousand times, and would tell herself a thousand more, but saying, wasn't the same as doing.

She fisted the check she found on her kitchen table. The edge of the paper cut into her palm as she marched into the barn looking for Blain. Her old boots thumped against the dirt while they ate up the distance between her bungalow and the stable.

When she turned the corner, she expected to find him but came upon a stranger reaching into the stall of her horse.

"Get away from there!"

Little Ms. Skinny Jeans and Plaid Shirt reached up to touch Pride, but she dropped her hand and backed away. "Sorry, I hoped to get to know her better before I strapped on the saddle and took her for a ride."

The woman's words were like a fist to Trinity's chin. Her head snapped back from the force.

"You're not saddling this horse. You sure as hell aren't

riding her." Trinity marched forward until she stood a foot away. "Who are you?"

The woman wiped her hands on her jeans before holding one out in greeting. "I'm Tracy Smith, the new horse trainer for Wallaby Ranch."

Tracy's words sent a sharp slice to Trinity's heart. Now she understood the reason the check said final pay.

"New trainer?"

"Yes, I arrived a few minutes ago and saw the barn. Thought I'd give the place a look before I talked to Blain about the details."

"Blain hired you?"

"Yes, he wants his daughter saddled with a winner." She opened her mouth to say something else, but Trinity turned and walked away. "Don't unpack, you're not staying. I'm the trainer here, and I don't need your help." She stomped out of the barn and up the hill to the house.

When she got to the large rancher with the wrap-around porch, she stopped, but only for a moment. It was customary to knock, but desperation coursed through her veins. Adrenaline rushed forth and made her burst uninvited through the front door.

"Blain Wallaby, where are you?" she yelled. She blazed from room to room until she found him in his office at the end of the hallway.

"I see you found your severance pay." He sat at the big desk with his boots kicked up to rest on the burled wood surface. His salt and pepper brows came into points in the center like he was sprouting horns. The man was Lucifer in a Stetson.

The check, in her hand, was all but forgotten until a paper cut sent a zing of discomfort up her arm. She unfurled her fist and dropped the slip of paper on his desk. The blood from the cut pinked her palm.

"We'll talk about the money in a second. What I want to know is why there's a woman named Tracy Smith in my barn? She says she's a new hire."

He kicked his feet off the desk and let his boots fall to the marble floor with a thud.

"Darlin', she is the new trainer. You tried and failed." He pointed to the chair in front of his desk.

She shook her head and stood her ground. She'd been in this position once too often. How many more times would she have to stand in front of a man while he told her she wasn't wanted or needed? The sad thing was, they always said it with a smile on their lips and a word of endearment spilling forth.

There was a time she loved to hear a man call her darlin'. That was before she realized that fifty percent of the time, it was condescending. *Darlin' get me a beer. Be a darlin' and sit on my lap. Oh, darlin', you thought I loved you?*

She crossed her arms over her chest and stomped her boot. "You brought me here to train your horses. I've done a great job with your stock." The sun peeked in the east-side window. Refractions of light danced around the room. "I'm happy where I am."

He smiled. "I'm not happy." He picked up the crumpled check and straightened it on the edge of the desk. "Angel still hasn't won a competition."

Trinity wanted to reach across and choke the man. "It's not about the horse." His daughter hadn't won because she had no skill. "Don't fire me, fire your daughter's trainer. Don't blame the horse when it's the rider."

"Have you seen Angel on a horse? She's a wonder to watch."

"Yes." Trinity rarely spoke out because no one listened, but she couldn't hold her tongue this time. "It's a wonder she can stay in the saddle."

He twisted his lips so tight they looked like a puckered anus. "And that's why you're leaving. You don't trust my judgment."

"You're right. I don't because it's clouded. When you look at Angel, you see a girl with unlimited possibilities. I applaud you for that. I wish my father had looked at me that way, but be realistic and take off the blinders. Horses are your thing, not hers. She'd rather be hanging out at the mall with her friends on the weekends. Instead, she's riding a horse she couldn't care less about."

"What do you know about my daughter?"

She wet her thumb and rubbed at the dried blood on her hand.

"Nothing really. Remember, I don't train her, I train her horse. But I was a daughter. Like Angel, I didn't have many choices, and I resent that to this day. How different would my life be if someone took the time to ask questions and listen?"

No one had ever asked what she wanted. Poor Angel was in the same saddle. With men like Blain Wallaby running the show, not much would change.

She picked up the check and shoved it in her back pocket. It wasn't much, but it would help.

"Your new trainer is in the stables."

It knotted her gut to be so easily replaced even though she knew without a doubt everyone was. Even her own mother had replaced her and her brothers with a new family when she left them and moved to Florida. Trinity was too young to remember, but she'd heard the stories of how Sally Mosier packed up the car on a snowy day. She climbed inside, started the engine, and left in search of sunshine.

"This isn't personal, Trinity."

"It is for me. You never came and talked to me. Never asked me what I thought about Angel and her chances of winning." She pointed at herself. "I trained champions before I came to work for you."

If she thought her insides were boiling earlier when Tracy touched her mare, she was on fire now.

"You're making a mistake. If you want Wallaby Ranch to have a win, I'll get back in the saddle and bring you one." She'd retired at twenty-eight. It wasn't the competition that did her in. It was the circuit. Constantly on the go with no place to land wasn't the life she dreamed about. At least working for Blain made her feel like she belonged somewhere, but she didn't. She never had, and she never would. That reality sat like a boulder on her chest.

He leaned his elbows on the desk and cradled his chin on the tops of his hands. "I'm sorry, Trinity."

She pressed her fingers against her temples, certain the throbbing was a sign her brain would explode.

"It would have been nice to have some warning. Where am I supposed to go?"

"Doesn't your father work at McKinley's?"

"Yes, he does." Blain didn't need to know she was persona non grata at that ranch. She'd left there years ago when another man not too different from Blain pointed at the door and told her to leave.

"You have options. You're good with horses. Surely someone can use you."

"Yep." She took a step back. "Someone always does." She patted the pocket holding the check. "How long do I have before you want me gone?"

He glanced out the window. "You've got until sunset. Tracy needs a place to sleep."

If a heart could tumble out of its bone enforced home, she was certain hers was in the toe of her boot. "What about my horse?"

He leaned back and chuckled. "Your horse?"

"You gave me Pride when my horse Bliss got put down. Pride is my horse."

He stood and walked toward her. "She was yours while you were here. You get to leave with what you came with."

She'd been compared to a storm at times. Her brothers called her a tornado. Right then, she could feel the force of her anger ratcheting up. The longer she stayed to argue her point, the less likely it would end well for either of them. "I'll be gone within the hour." She turned on her heel and strode to the door but stopped and looked over her shoulder. "You'll be begging me to come back."

He tipped up his chin to dismiss her. "We'll see."

Each step she took weighted her down. The goodbyes always gutted her. The last time she said goodbye, it was to her father and her brother Cade. She left McKinley Ranch not because she wanted to but because someone had lied, and everyone believed them.

She reached the barn and followed the ray of sun that led her through the door on a direct path to Pride.

Tracy leaned against the wall, waiting. "Did you get it all straightened out?"

Trinity gave her a sideways glance and nodded. She

focused on her horse. "Hey, sweetheart." The dappled mare nuzzled her neck. "Looks like I have to go." She moved to Angel's horse, Triumph, and turned to Tracy. "She's got a suspensory ligament injury on the front right. Rest, ice, and compression is what she needs, not more training."

Trinity moved back to Pride because leaving her was equal to abandoning a child. She was well versed on that subject. She kissed the muzzle of the horse she thought of as hers and walked away. Several minutes later, she entered her home—a guesthouse on the property that sat several hundred yards from the bunkhouse.

She pulled her suitcase from the closet, laid it open on the bed, and searched her drawers.

Blain's words rang in her ears. "You can leave with what you came with." The drawers overflowed with clothes. Things she hadn't purchased herself but gifts she'd received since her arrival. She dug through the neatly folded piles and found nothing from her past.

The only items that were rightly hers were the boots on her feet, the hat hanging from the bedpost, and an oiled jacket she'd brought from Wyoming.

She closed the suitcase and pushed it to the hardwood floor. She picked up her backpack and filled it with her toiletries and two pictures she had on her dresser before heading out the front door.

Standing on her porch was Trigger. She didn't know his real name, but he'd been at the ranch long before she arrived.

"I see you're heading out."

She wanted to cry, but she'd learned long ago that tears never helped. "My replacement showed up."

"Come next month, you'll be one of his many regrets. Where you headed?"

Months ago, she wouldn't have known, but that was before both of her brothers settled in a small Colorado town called Aspen Cove.

"I'm heading north. Do you think you can give me a ride to the bus station?" She had limited funds. She'd never been much of a saver; then again, she didn't earn much to save. When her SUV broke down, Blain gave her a ranch truck to use. At the time, he appeared to be her chance at freedom, but he was just a stopgap to this point in her life.

"I always knew Wallaby Ranch wouldn't suit you long-term. You're too good for us." He gently took her elbow and led her behind the bunkhouse, where they stored the old equipment. He walked to a tarp-covered vehicle and yanked the fabric off.

She gasped. "My SUV." Surprise filled her voice. "How? I thought Blain had it hauled away."

His gummy smile warmed her. Trigger could have been anywhere between forty and a hundred. With his sun-leathered skin and his salt and pepper hair, it was difficult to tell.

"He told me to do something with it. I did. I fixed it up and stored it away until you needed it." He reached into the open window. When he lowered the visor, the keys dropped out. "You climb in and find somewhere to belong. Someplace where people know your value."

She found it ironic that he knew exactly what her heart longed for. A place to fit in.

She tossed her backpack into the passenger seat before she threw her arms around him for a hug. "You were always good to me, Trigger."

"Darlin', you're the daughter I never had." He opened the door, and she climbed inside.

When she turned the key, her old beat-up 4Runner purred to life. "You're my hero."

He shook his head. "Nope, I'm just a man who wants to do right by you."

"You'd be the first," she said and fastened her seatbelt.

She drove out of the old barn. The dirt road wound around the acreage until she hit the highway. She took one last glance in her rearview mirror. Texas would soon be behind her.

She didn't call her brothers to tell them she was on her way. It would give them too much time to hide or move.

She turned on the radio and headed north.

"Aspen Cove, here I come."

CHAPTER TWO

Wyatt Morrison was a lot of things, but he wasn't stupid. He never mixed business with pleasure. A man didn't get where he wanted to be if there was a woman in his path waiting to trip him up.

"Do we understand each other?" Lloyd asked.

"We understood each other weeks ago when you sent me to live at Cade's ranch. I'm not interested in your daughter. Never have been, and never will be."

Lloyd nodded and walked out, leaving him alone to care for both horses.

"Why the hell did I sign up for this shit?" He offered water to Lloyd's horse first, then moved to Rex. "I thought things would be different for us." He pulled off his gelding's saddle and brushed him down. Rex had been with him for years and was a good listener. "I came here for an opportunity. Look at where I'm at now." He finished grooming his horse, then moved him into a stall where fresh water and hay waited.

He tugged on the reins of Lloyd's horse, Hellion, and moved him closer so he could brush him down. He grabbed the bucket of grooming supplies and got started.

"Maybe I should have stayed in Montana." He moved the brush over Hellion's coat and growled. The sound startled the horse, who sidestepped him as if trying to escape.

"I get it. You don't want to be here either."

Wyatt had moved from Bozeman when he heard about the job in Aspen Cove. A small cattle farmer named Lloyd Dawson was looking to expand and needed a righthand man. That meant he wanted a foreman, which was all Wyatt wanted to be. It wasn't Lloyd's fault Wyatt hadn't asked the right questions, or enough questions. He had been ready to leave Montana and jumped at the first chance he got.

He'd packed up his things and moved to Aspen Cove to make his mark on the world, but things at the Big D Ranch weren't exactly as he'd hoped.

"Hey, man." Basil, or Baz as he preferred to be called, moved his horse inside the stable. "Thought you'd have left by now."

"I'll be gone as soon as I'm done grooming Hellion."

"That used to be my job." He chuckled. "That is until you came along."

"Yep, earning my keep."

"Hardly. If you ask me, I think you're getting the prickly point of the stirrup."

The kid was right. That was another piece of information Wyatt didn't have until he drove onto the ranch. Lloyd had a son. A son who was the acting foreman. It chapped his ass to fall under the supervision of a kid who was barely out of diapers when Wyatt made his first cattle drive.

"It's all good." It wasn't, but work was work, and until something better came along, he'd have to tolerate the situation.

"You mind grooming Titan when you're finished with Hellion?" Baz looked at the clock hanging from the barn wall. "I've got a class at Dalton's. We're making chicken cordon bleu tonight, and I don't want to be late."

"It's fine. Tie him off, and I'll get to him next." All that waited for him was a silent cabin and a canned meal.

"Thanks, man." Baz took off like a bullet shot from a pistol.

Wyatt finished Hellion and put him in his stall before bringing Titan inside the barn.

"I'm a glorified stable boy."

"You're far more than that." Violet walked in, sipping sweet tea. He knew it was sweet because she used to bring him one each night after he came in from the range.

"What are you doing here?" She was a pretty girl, but a girl. "Does your daddy know you're in the stables?" Trouble came in all kinds of packages. Sadly, this bundle was the boss's youngest daughter.

She laughed. "I haven't called him Daddy for years. And hell no. If he did, I'd have a sore ass, and you'd have a hole in your chest. Daddy," she said with a hint of sarcasm, "doesn't leave his shotgun on the porch as a warning. He puts it there because it's efficient. All he needs to do is lean down and pick it up. It's already cocked and ready to go."

She closed the distance between them. She'd been hot for him since he arrived. On that first day, he'd no sooner saddled his horse when she offered to let him ride her instead.

The way her cheeks turned crimson made him embarrassed for her. Hearing those words come out of her mouth was like listening to porn recited by Mother Theresa—just wrong.

"Go back to the house before you get in trouble and get me fired."

She inched closer. "Maybe I like trouble."

He hopped back. "Well, I don't. I need this job, so stay away. I'm old enough to be your father." He was if he'd had her at eighteen.

She set her hands on her hips. "Hardly. Even if you were, I prefer my men older and with more experience."

He bent over and picked up the bucket of water. "Go home, Violet. You don't ride a bull before you've ridden a horse." He poured the bucket onto the ground, splashing her.

She sprang back. "That's a ridiculous analogy. Everyone starts somewhere. Some of us refuse to start at the beginning."

He walked Baz's horse into his stall to get him settled for the night. When he came out, he moved straight toward his truck. "Have a good night."

"You're such an ass, Wyatt."

He lifted his hand in a backward wave. "Glad we agree on something."

He left the ranch, moving at twice the speed limit. "If Lloyd doesn't paddle that girl's bottom, I might have to," he said to no one. He shook that thought from his head. "Hell, she'd probably like it."

It was a thirty-minute drive to where he bunked. Thankfully Cade had given him a place to stay as long as he helped set up the bunkhouse. He was the only one living in the place, but if Cade kept increasing his livestock, he'd need help soon. Maybe he could bring him on board. At least he wouldn't be risking life and limb each time he went to work. Next time he saw the man, he'd ask.

When he pulled in front of the cabin, he didn't go in right away. On days like today, when he felt trapped, he liked to sit in the open on the rock above the pond and count the minnows.

He was up to ninety-eight when hooves coming from his left broke the silence. Off in the distance, he watched Cade's horse canter toward him.

"How's it going, Wyatt?"

They didn't see each other much, but with the days getting longer and the sun setting later, that might change.

"Good, just unwinding. This is a good place to let the weight of the day fall off my shoulders."

Cade swung from his saddle and walked over to sit on a nearby rock. "I used to bathe in this pond." He pointed toward his tiny airstream trailer. "It's got everything but a shower I can fit in."

Hard to believe he'd lived in the tiny tow-behind. Harder to believe that in a period of a few months, he'd gone from living there to living with the pretty beekeeper.

"How's Abby?" Wyatt had seen the two together. Rumor had it that Cade was fire, and she was gasoline, but all he saw was smoldering love. "I see she hasn't killed you yet."

Cade picked up a rock and skipped it across the surface of the water. "I'm her official bear killer, so I have a purpose. What about you? You got a girl somewhere?"

How long had it been since he'd had a lady in his life? A year? Two? The life of a cattleman wasn't glamorous. There were long days followed by lonely nights. Most women wouldn't put up with giving a lot to get a little. At the end of the day, he had limited energy and money to offer. Women in the twenty-first century were looking for more than love. Sometimes love didn't even enter the equation.

"Nope. Women are problematic. You don't even have to look at them, and you get booted off the ranch."

Cade laughed. "All Lloyd has left is his five daughters and a son who cooks better than any woman I know." He glanced over his shoulder. "Don't tell Abby I said that, or she'll have me sleeping in the bunkhouse again."

Wyatt leaned back and looked at the sky. The sun was setting, and an orange glow lit the horizon.

"I love it here, but it's not panning out to be what I hoped for."

"Give it a chance. You might change your mind. Small-town life is tough to get used to, but it will grow on you."

It wasn't small-town living that drove him nuts. Small-town thinking did the trick. Working on a ranch where the owner thought he would steal everything, including his annoying daughter, was a challenge. He'd heard how the last foreman took everything, but Wyatt wasn't that guy, and he refused to pay the price for another man's misdeeds.

"Why did you leave Wyoming?" Wyatt asked. He knew Cade came from a horse ranch, although he preferred cattle. Who wouldn't? Horses were like women. They needed a lot of attention. Cattle went about their day, not caring if you paid them any mind.

"I left McKinley Ranch because I wanted more," Cade said.

"There's nothing wrong with more." He wanted more too. He had the skill to run a ranch but never the seniority or the money to start his own.

"I wish I would have known you were unhappy at Big D's." Cade chuckled. It was hard not to when saying the name of Lloyd's ranch. "I would have hired you here. As it is, someone is coming from the McKinley ranch to help me out. I'm growing faster than expected. It's too big for one man to manage."

"Always a day late and a dollar short." He blew out his frustration in a sigh.

"You'll figure it out."

Wyatt sat up and rolled to his feet. "That I will. The only thing I have to figure out today is if I want stew or chili for dinner."

Cade's phone rang. He held up a finger as if asking Wyatt to wait. He answered on the second ring. "Miss me already?" Seconds later, he growled at the phone. "Don't tell me, Angie is back."

Wyatt brushed the dust from his jeans and watched Cade plead.

"Abby, I swear there's no one else."

Cade looked at Wyatt and lifted his shoulders. "What does she look like?" They both turned to look at the white SUV in the distance.

Abby gave him an answer that had Cade responding with a cross between a laugh and a choke.

"Before you shoot her, ask her name."

The next thing Wyatt saw was Cade running to his horse. "Holy shit. Close the door and lock it. Tell her I've moved." He whipped the reins around. "Sweetheart, you pegged her right. She's trouble. Like a seismic ten on the Richter scale. Or a category five hurricane."

Cade hung up. "I have to go."

"Trouble?"

"Yes. My sister's here."

CHAPTER THREE

"Thanks for inviting me in. No doubt your hospitality won't be popular with my brother."

"He doesn't have a say so. This is my house."

"Well, that was a smart move. If I had resources, I'd have a house too, but sadly I've never had a permanent place to call home." That wasn't an exaggeration. Home had always been wherever their father worked.

Abby waved her in. "Come on. He's on his way."

Trinity didn't know the woman Cade had chosen. She only knew her brother had fallen hard. Abby wasn't his normal type, but maybe that was the attraction. There was something prickly about her that lay under the surface. Something that felt familiar, as if she'd experienced the same pain. Maybe heartache was universal. In her case, it wasn't over a man. Not really. This time it was over losing Pride. Not her own, but the mare she'd grown to love. During the trip from Texas to Colorado, she'd thought of at least a dozen ways to torture Blain for his cruelty. When she imagined sticking a cattle prod up his ass, she shuddered and let the thoughts go.

"Thank you." Trinity's heart felt like it was on a horse rounding a barrel with the way it moved inside her chest. She entered the warm and cozy cabin and glanced around. It didn't have the high-end finishes that made Blain's feel like a homestead built for Hollywood, but instead looked like a cabin that grew up with the land. "This is lovely. Have you lived here all your life?"

Abby laughed. "No, but this house and land have been in my family for hundreds of years." She pointed toward the door. "The Coolidges owned the land across the way, the acreage where your brother is building his ranch, but that's a long story. It was basically the Hatfields and McCoys, but instead of a pig, it was cattle and water that started the war. In my family's case, only one person died."

In Trinity's mind or at least her experience, there was little in life to fight for. "That sounds awful."

"Tea? I have fresh honey." Abby pointed to the kitchen table and set the instant kettle to boil.

"You raise bees, right?"

"I do, although I'm not sure you can call it raising them. They do all the work, and now that your brother built a fence around the property to keep out other wildlife, there isn't much for me to do except sit back and wait. Harvest time isn't until the fall. While they do their thing, I'm learning how to ride a horse and get used to the smell of a T-bone steak in the making." She scrunched her nose. "I prefer the after product."

She couldn't remember exactly what she'd heard about Abby. None of it came from Cade because they didn't chat that often. Her brother Luke only called if he needed a woman's perspective. Most of her insider information came from their father. He was the reason Trinity was taking a chair at Abby's table. If she didn't talk to him on the regular, she wouldn't know anything about her brothers.

When the pot whistled, Abby brought it to the table and pulled out several canisters of loose tea, a honeypot, and two strainers. The teacups sitting in front of them were the real deal, with saucers and all.

"You go big for your tea." Trinity chose the English breakfast tea even though it was evening. Completely skipping over the next few hours and moving straight to tomorrow morning sounded appealing.

"I love a great cup of tea. What makes it better is a helping of honey." She took the honeypot and removed the dipper, letting the amber liquid trickle into the hot tea. "You know what goes even better with tea?" Abby asked.

"No, but I bet you'll tell me."

"Gossip. Fill me in on everything about Cade that he wouldn't share himself." She laughed. "Not the dirty details, but the fun stuff about him as a kid."

She'd barely opened her mouth when the door flung open, and he stomped inside. The one thing about the Mosiers was they were the calm in the storm until they became the storm. By the look in his eyes, he was building up to be a doozy.

Trinity rose from her seat and walked over to him. Despite his I'm-going-to-kill you look, she kissed his cheek. "Hey, big brother. I've missed you."

He pointed to the door. "Out."

She shook her head. "Is that any way to greet me? I haven't seen you in two years." The last time she'd seen him, Cade and her father were delivering a horse to

Wallaby Ranch for Angel. The same horse Trinity had trained.

Cade looked from her to Abby. "You're right." He drew her into his arms and gave her a bear hug. After several seconds, he stepped back, pointed at the exit, and said, "Out."

Abby, despite her size, was next to them in a few strides. She stood in front of Cade. "Don't forget this is my house, and while I love sharing it with you, you don't get to decide who stays and who goes."

Trinity watched her brother get smaller with each of Abby's words. It was funny how the right person could influence everything.

"You're right, sweetheart, but I'm trying to protect what we have. Every penny I've got is invested in that ranch." He turned to Trinity. "She's a damn hurricane. A reckless tornado. A tsunami. Everywhere she goes becomes her next disaster."

Trinity fisted her hips. "Not true. If you ever took the time to weigh the facts, you'd know that listening to others is a waste of time. What's worse is you never listened to me, and I'm family. We share DNA."

He nodded. "I've heard too many tales to discount them all. One story yes, two maybe, but when everyone tells the same tail, it's hard to refute." His voice rose with each word. "You don't get to come here and wreak havoc. I won't let you put an end to what I'm starting."

She growled and stomped her boots. "The only havoc I'll create is the disappearance of your body. If I were a guy, everything that happened wouldn't be an issue. Two girls fight over a guy, and he's a stud. Same thing happens to me, and I'm a whore. It only becomes an issue because I have a vagina."

"Not true, and I never said you were a whore. I've only said you were trouble." He crossed his arms over his chest.

Abby stepped back and leaned on the sofa. The smile pulling at her lips told Trinity she was enjoying this sibling argument.

"It is true. If it wasn't, how come I was the only one that had to leave when shit hit the fan in Wyoming?"

"You caused the problem."

"Because I was a female."

"This isn't up for debate. Three guys laid down fists over you."

"You're right, but no one asked why; they just assumed I created the issue. I didn't come here because I wanted to. I came here because I had no other choice." She hated being forced to crawl back to family. At thirty, she should have been able to care for herself. She was a hard worker and a good trainer, but room and board plus a small monthly stipend didn't afford her many options.

"What happened in Texas?" Cade asked. "I thought things were going well."

She shrugged. "They were until he fired me."

Cade scrubbed his face with both hands. "See, you're trouble wherever you go."

"You know what? Coming home to family was the worst decision." She turned to Abby. "You wanted some inside information?" She pointed to her brother. "Look at him. He'd sell me to the Taliban before he took me in."

Cade marched toward the refrigerator and grabbed a beer. He popped the top and took a long drink. "If I sold you to terrorists, they'd agree to peace in order for us to take you back."

"Fine." She walked to the table and picked up her

purse. She returned to Abby. "Thank you for the tea and your kindness." She pointed to her brother. "Big animals are hard to train, so I wish you luck."

She moved to the door.

"Wait," Abby called after her. "Don't leave."

"Abby," Cade said. "It's me or Trinity. You choose because we can't both live in your house."

Abby frowned. "I'm sorry you feel that way, Cade, because I love you, but I also know you'll be okay on your own. I'd like to get to know your sister better." She looked at Trinity. "You want to stay the night?"

After spending sixteen hours in her SUV, a bed was all she wanted. But by nature, she wasn't a mischief-maker. "I appreciate the offer, but I didn't come here to cause problems. I'll sleep in my car."

Abby moved quickly to block her exit. "No. You'll sleep here. Cade can sleep in the bunkhouse."

"I what?"

Abby opened the door. "You heard me." She pointed toward the porch. "Out."

"But Abby," he pleaded.

"No buts. I don't know who you are if you can turn your back on your sister. Family is everything. Seems to me, like you might need to have a night alone to think about it." At just over five feet tall, Abby poked against Cade's six-foot frame until he stepped out the door, and she closed it. "Now, where were we?"

Trinity couldn't move. She'd never had anyone choose her blindly. Right then, she knew Abby was an ally.

"Tea, we were drinking tea."

"Yes, and you were telling me stuff about Cade."

Trinity went back to the table and took a seat. Physically and emotionally drained, her energy faded, and all she wanted was a soft bed and ten hours of sleep. Given that Abby had gifted her with kindness, she was happy to share a few memories. She wasn't much of a storyteller. She'd learned early on that no matter what she said, whether it was the truth or a lie, no one believed her. The men in her family jumped to conclusions first. If her father had his stories straight, her brother Luke had done the same with his girl Riley when he accused her of being an arsonist. She wondered what Cade had thought of Abby at the start. No doubt, his initial impressions were far from accurate.

"I'm not much of a storyteller, but I've got a few tales to share." Trinity had Abby laughing by the time she finished.

"I know he's afraid of bees, but I didn't know he feared spiders. He's frightened by dragonflies too?"

Trinity giggled. "Yep, he says they're the scorpions of the skies."

"What about you?" Abby rose from the table and dished up the pasta and sauce that was simmering on the stovetop. "What are you afraid of?"

Trinity sipped her tea. "Never belonging anywhere." She hadn't expected to be so open about her feelings. Maybe she let her guard down because she was tired, or maybe it was Abby who made her feel safe to share something personal.

"You are Cade's family, and you belong here." Abby set a plate of spaghetti with meat sauce in front of her. "Eat up, and then I'll show you where you're sleeping."

"Are you sure? Really, this should be Cade sitting here and not me." She looked down at the home-cooked meal and sighed. She couldn't remember the last time a woman had cared for her or fed her a meal. All the ranches she'd worked had men in charge. They were managed by men, with rules made for them. It was always a man who cooked for the bunkhouse. In Dallas, she got her meals from Trigger. They were nothing special, usually a slab of meat and a baked potato.

Sitting in front of a plate of spaghetti was up there with gold nuggets, unicorns, and babies' smiles. Tears pooled in her eyes, but she willed them back because Trinity Mosier cried for no one.

CHAPTER FOUR

Wyatt was a restless soul, which is what made him jump from location to location. He was searching for something he couldn't define but knew he'd recognize when it appeared. That knowing wasn't coming from Big D.

A stomping sound on the porch drew his attention. The door swung open, and in walked Cade.

"You need something?"

Cade tossed his jacket on the sofa. "I need a meal and a beer."

Wyatt didn't get visitors. Especially men who ate home-cooked meals made by little beekeepers. "Trouble in paradise? Abby hear you say Baz cooked better than her?"

"No. It's not that." Cade walked to the refrigerator and looked inside. "One beer, man? That's all you got?" He slammed the door and stomped into the living area. "Grab whatever you need so we can leave for the brew-house. Beers on me. Ears on you. I've got to vent."

Wyatt never turned down free booze. He picked up

his keys and chased Cade outside. He found him already seated on the passenger side of his truck.

"I guess I'm driving." Wyatt climbed into the cab and turned toward town. "You want to start now? I have a feeling this is going to be a long story."

Cade leaned back and tilted his face to the ceiling. "Women are too damn hard to figure out." He threw his hands in the air. "I killed a damn bear for her, and she chose my sister over me."

Wyatt snapped his attention toward Cade. "Chose how? Like she's switching teams?"

"No." He pointed to the road. "Watch where you're going. I want to get drunk, not dead."

"Fine. You're buying; I'm driving. You think Cannon will have some pizza at the brewhouse?"

"He always does," Cade grumbled, as he said something about women under his breath. "I should be there, eating spaghetti tonight. Do you know how good Abby's pasta is?"

"Not a clue, but if you're whining, it must be amazing." The last Italian food he'd had was from a can. Once he'd doctored it with parmesan cheese, it wasn't half bad. He was certain the tiny meatballs were rabbit poop disguised as meat, but he'd had worse.

"So, is this about your sister?"

"You had to ruin a moment, didn't you?"

"Just peeling back the onion to get to the center." He turned onto Main Street and found a parking spot right in front of Bishop's Brewhouse.

"I don't like onions, and I'm not a current fan of my sister."

They exited the truck and entered. Monday nights weren't busy until football season.

Cannon stood behind the bar. His cat Mike lay across the old-fashioned register swishing his tail over the keys. "Single or a pitcher?" he asked.

Cade raised two fingers. "I'll need two ... pitchers and Dalton's pizza if you got it."

"No pizza," Cannon said. "I've got bar mix." He looked at the clock on the wall. "You can probably squeeze an order in at Maisey's before she closes. How about two burgers and fries?"

Cade nodded and held up a twenty. Cannon rushed by to grab it. He dropped off the beer and continued straight out the door.

"I love this town," Wyatt said. "It's like a wish factory."

Cade laughed. "You want a wish, go to the bakery. The bar is for realists and fatalists."

"And antagonists, which is what I'd say you were since you got kicked out of the house."

The sound of pool balls broke, and Wyatt turned to face the bikers who'd taken up residence there. If you wanted to know anything about the town you were in, all you needed to do was hang out a few evenings at the local watering hole. It wasn't odd to find the rough-looking bunch in the brewhouse. They'd been friends of Dalton's before he did his stint in prison. He learned about Dalton first because, by definition, he was a murderer, and he married a famous pop star who went by the name Indigo. If a murderer could marry a rich pop music artist, then he could reach his goal. All he wanted was a satisfying work experience, an occasional good meal, and a roll in the hay from time to time. Was that too much to hope for?

"Trinity is trouble tripled."

Wyatt poured them a mug of beer. He watched as Cade drank his first without a breath.

"All right, give me the condensed version before our meal comes."

"She's a pain in the ass."

"She's your sister, so that's a prerequisite. I've got a sister too, but she lives too far away to be my problem."

"See, you've got it right. When you have a sibling like Trinity, you need a few states in between as a buffer."

"That doesn't tell me about her. Give me five words that describe her."

Cade poured himself another beer. "Hurricane. Tornado. Earthquake. Tsunami. Trouble."

"She can't be that bad."

"You don't understand. She nearly got us all kicked off McKinley Ranch."

"Why?"

"I'm not dredging that up again. It gives me indigestion."

"Okay. If I weigh things out, they're never as bad as I thought. For example, my experience at the Big D isn't great. I've got no upward mobility, the man trusts no one, I can't live there, there's Violet who's like gum on my shoe, and Lloyd has a shotgun by the door. But ... he's got longhorns, and the range is beautiful. He is generous with his time, the weather shelters are fully stocked, and the pay is decent. Now, tell me five things about Trinity that will even the scales."

Cade sucked down a half mug of suds. "She's great with horses."

"That's one. Keep going."

"She keeps to herself."

Wyatt frowned. How did someone who kept to herself cause disruption? "What else?"

"She's tidy and cleans up after everyone."

"Sounds like a damn saint." Wyatt lifted his mug and took a drink.

Cade shook his head. "No way. That's part of the problem. Everyone falls in love with her, and if rumors are true, she loves everyone. I mean everyone, man."

"Oh, so she starts fights among the men?"

"Yep, and I don't need those problems on my ranch."

Cannon opened the door and plopped the two to-go containers on the counter. "You want the change?"

Cade waved him off. "You keep it."

"Thanks, I'll need it." Without an invitation to join them, Cannon pulled a chair out, turned it around, and straddled it. "No repeating what I'm about to tell you until Sage breaks the news, but I knocked her up."

Wyatt was still too new in town to understand the significance of that. He wasn't sure if it was a good thing or something he should offer his condolences for.

"No way." Cade slapped him on the back. "When is the critter due?"

"Thanksgiving time, but say nothing to no one, or I'll be sleeping on the porch."

Wyatt busted out in a laugh. "Is that a thing here? Your women get mad and toss you out on your ass."

Cannon stared at Cade. "Abby kick you out?" A laugh rolled through him. "Big bad cowboy gets bested by a beekeeper."

Cade popped a fry into his mouth. "Better than getting laid out by a leprechaun. I'd put my money on Sage any day."

Cannon's smile faded. "You know it, but a wise man

29

realizes when he's outsmarted, and that woman had my number the minute she met me."

"You too?" Wyatt shook his head. "How long did it take for your women to whip you into shape?"

Cannon stood and tucked the chair back under the table. "I'm still in training. Then again, I like her whip." He walked to the pool table and picked up the empty mugs.

"What about you?" Cade asked. "No one to make you feel shitty about yourself or remind you you're not the god you think you are?"

"I don't need a woman to beat me up for my choices," Wyatt said. "I can do that on my own. Almost wish I could blame it on someone else, but I leaped before I looked this time."

"Sometimes, the leap is worth the risk of landing wrong." Cade picked up his burger and took a bite. After he swallowed, he continued. "I didn't know what I was getting into when I purchased the land sight unseen. I trusted my brother to not lead me astray. I'd say I ended up in a sweet position. But don't forget, Abby tried to burn me out before she let me in. She stole my clothes, wouldn't remove a beehive in the bunkhouse, and tried to get me eaten by a bear. I wouldn't say what I have has come easy, but it was worth it."

"Even though you'll be bunking with me tonight?"

"Yep, because tomorrow, I'll get in her good graces and ... make-up sex is amazing."

They finished their meals, and Cade drank the second pitcher of beer by himself.

It was a wobbly walk to the truck. Once Wyatt poured Cade into the passenger seat, he started for home. Funny how the bunkhouse had become his home. Then again, home was where he kicked off his boots and hung his hat.

"You're getting a roommate tomorrow," Cade slurred.

"Your sister?"

Cade weaved back and forth in his seat. "No, I've got that guy coming from Wyoming."

"What's he like?" It didn't much matter because they wouldn't be working together. Wyatt was an outsider. He didn't work Cade's ranch, only bedded there.

"He's a cowboy, so he's an asshole." Cade laughed. "What do you think of calling the ranch the Big C?"

"I'd rethink that. Putting the Big C next to the Big D is a mistake."

"Not usually, but you're probably right. I should revisit my naming strategy when I'm sober."

Wyatt pulled in front of the bunkhouse. He climbed out of the truck while Cade fell out.

"I'm okay." He hopped to his feet and headed to the trailer. "I'll bunk in here."

Wyatt watched him stumble toward the door. "That's why I don't have a woman. No one's kicking me out of my house. I mean really, how much trouble can your sister be?"

"I'll introduce you to her tomorrow before she's on her way out of town." He opened the door and stepped inside the gleaming silver bullet. "I'm telling you, my sister is trouble."

He walked toward the bunkhouse. What did Trinity's kind of trouble look like? Was she mouthy, sassy trouble? Long legged, big busted trouble? A woman he didn't know was trouble until the morning after?

Would she be a mug of beer problem or a two-pitcher number like Abby? Wyatt headed straight for the refrigerator and took the last beer out. He went to the porch and leaned over the rail, looking toward Abby's cabin. The guest room light was on.

"What are you doing over there, Trinity?" He twisted the cap off the beer and closed his eyes, trying to imagine what a sister of Luke and Cade Mosier was like. Putting a rack on Cade made him want to puke. Putting heels and a dress on Luke brought out the same reaction. He drank his beer and headed for bed. Tomorrow was a new beginning. As intriguing as meeting Trinity sounded, he wasn't looking for trouble. There was no need to seek it out. Trouble always found its way to him.

CHAPTER FIVE

Trinity didn't need an alarm to wake her. She'd been rising with the sun since she was born. She sat on the edge of the bed and pulled on her jeans and then her boots.

She needed a plan. If things didn't work out at Cade's, she wasn't sure what she'd do. She stood, peeled back the curtain and peeked outside. The new day rose from the field's edge. Pressing her cheek against the cold glass, she closed her eyes and said a prayer. "Dear Lord, let today go better than yesterday."

The smell of coffee guided her to the kitchen, where Abby was pouring two mugs. "Saw the light on under the door. Thought you'd be joining me." She passed off one mug and sat at the table. "How did you sleep?"

"Better than I've slept in a while. Must be the cold night air or the altitude."

Abby uncovered a basket of muffins. "Or you feel safe. You're with family now."

Trinity choked on her coffee. "That's an odd word pairing for me."

"I have a sister, but she lives far away. I would love it if she moved back to Aspen Cove."

"You're lucky to have a sibling you like."

Abby slathered her muffin with butter and drizzled honey on next. "You don't like Cade?"

"I do. I think he's amazing. Watch how a man treats his horse, and you'll know how he treats his woman. I'm sure he's wonderful to you. I'm his sister, and it's different for me." She shrugged and picked at the muffin. "Did you make these?"

"No changing the subject."

"Fine. I love both my brothers, and I'm sure they love me, but it hasn't been easy." She pulled a raisin from the top of the muffin and set it aside. She wasn't a fan of them. "Our mother abandoned us when I was a baby. Dad, Luke, and Cade raised me. They expect me to be a certain way." How did she explain that to Abby when she hardly could process it herself? They'd raised her to be one of the guys.

Abby took a bite and chewed slowly. "I know your brother enough to know he's a cinderblock with women. Chip at him long enough, and you'll get inside."

Trinity laughed. "Oh, so you do know him." She bit the muffin, ignoring the foul taste of the raisins. "Did you say you made these?"

"No, I get them at the bakery. Those are from yesterday. Katie has a muffin schedule. Mondays are carrot cake. They're my favorite. Now back to your brother."

"I don't want to cause problems. It's never been my intention, but somehow trouble follows me. I'm a hard worker. I'm not mouthy with anyone, but my brothers. They treat me like one of the guys. That is until someone figures out I'm not."

Abby laughed. "That's the problem."

"I know, but I have to be one of the guys to earn my place."

Abby rose to get the coffeepot and topped off their mugs. "Have you looked in the mirror lately?"

"Every day, and every day I hate myself even more."

"You're beautiful. Not to sound creepy or anything, but most girls would have a crush on you. If your brother thinks you can blend in with the guys, then he's a bigger idiot than I thought."

Trinity rarely wore makeup. In fact, her beauty go-to was a tube of Chapstick. She'd considered shaving off her long blonde hair once but didn't think she could pull off the look, so she opted for a ponytail most days.

"I don't want to be the girl who says it's a curse to be pretty because that makes me sound like an idiot. Being pretty is not all that and a candy bar."

"The incident in Wyoming. Do you want to talk about it?"

Talking to Abby was easy, but what good would it do to pick at the scabs of old wounds?

"Not really. Let's just say that everyone there saw it differently than I did. I was fighting for my right to make a choice, and I lost my ability to choose anything at all." She stood and took her empty coffee mug to the sink. "That's not exactly true. I chose the direction I drove. It's how I ended up in Texas."

She picked up her purse and walked to the door. "Abby, thank you for letting me stay."

"Whoa, wait a minute. You can't leave until your brother gets back. We can work this out." She rushed forward to stand in front of Trinity. Abby took her phone

35

from her pocket and dialed. "Cade, it's time for you to come home and talk."

"It's best if I leave." Trinity leaned against the couch, hoping Abby would step aside. She was a tiny little thing. There was no doubt she could muscle her way past Abby, but for what reason? If she wanted her to stay for a few more minutes, she could. She was in no hurry to get anywhere and had no place to go.

Five minutes later, Cade walked inside. He looked at her and turned toward Abby, who had taken a seat on the sofa.

He dropped to his knees in front of Abby. "I missed you."

Trinity wanted to roll her eyes and say something snarky, but she didn't. A girl needed to know when to speak up and when to shut up. That had been her problem in Wyoming. She'd opened her mouth.

"Do you want me to wait outside while you lovebirds make up?"

Cade took a seat next to Abby and waved Trinity over.

Three was a crowd, so she took the chair in the corner. "Contrary to popular belief, I didn't come here to ruin anything for you."

He tucked his chin. "I know. You came here because you were desperate."

His wording irked her despite its accuracy.

"I have no plans to stay. I need a place to regroup and figure out my next step. I couldn't go to Dad. Luke and I aren't as close as you and me. I thought I could count on my big brother." She played with the frayed end of her T-shirt. "I was wrong. I put too much value on us being related."

She watched as Abby elbowed him in the side.

"Trin, I love you. I do, but whether or not you're looking for it, shit happens when you're around. You're too damn pretty and too damn smart for your own good."

She stared straight ahead. She'd become a master at hiding her emotions. No one she'd ever been around had the tolerance for tears or tantrums. Both of which she could let loose at any moment.

"If I didn't know you so well, I'd find that insulting," she said. "Since when did being smart become a problem?"

Abby elbowed him again.

Cade turned to her. "What?"

Her smile was as sweet as her honey. "You have about two seconds to offer her a place to stay. If you don't, I will, and you know what that means for you. Should I pack your stuff?"

If the situation wasn't so serious, Trinity would have laughed. Who would have thought a woman much smaller in stature, but twice his size in courage, could bring her brother to his knees?

"You can stay, but not in the main house. There's a trailer and a bunkhouse. The choice is yours. Get a job and figure out your long-term plans."

She replayed his words. "I can stay?"

He pointed to the front door. "Yes, but the accommodations are rough."

This time she laughed. "Don't forget, I've lived in bunkhouses all my life."

"Look for employment in town. Tourist season is starting. Maybe the bakery or the diner can hire you."

Her mouth dropped open. "To do what? All I know is horses."

"They don't serve them in town. Put those looks and that brain to use, or you'll starve."

Abby pinched his thigh. "Or she can care for your horses, and you'll feed her until she finds something else."

He made a sound like he was clearing his throat. "Fine, you manage my stable, and I'll make sure the pantry is stocked. You can cook, right?"

"You got a microwave?"

"Nope, but there are a couple of pans and a range. You'll figure it out."

She would. She'd learned to be resourceful. "Thank you for the reprieve. I promise to not be a pain."

"Good luck with that." He stood and walked over to her. "Now give me a hug, and tell me what you've been up to."

She held on to him for a long minute before stepping to the side. "There isn't much to tell. Ended up in Texas working for Blain until he fired me."

"Because you slept with him, and it didn't work out."

"Why is that every man's go-to as an excuse? Besides, you have to know his junk doesn't work. Not that I tried it on for size, but he got castrated by that bull five years ago. You have to remember that story. It's why his wife left."

Cade cupped his junk. "Yep. Wasn't sure it was true, though." He appeared uncomfortable with talk of another man's jewels.

"I wouldn't know from experience, but I'd say he's a eunuch. He didn't fire me because of sex. He fired me because he's an idiot. He blamed his daughter's failure to win on the horse."

"Any truth to that?" Cade asked.

"Seriously?" Trinity groaned. "I trained those horses. They'd win without a rider but stick someone who'd rather be somewhere else on their back, and it's a recipe for disaster. He's a typical man. He decided what Angel wanted. He never asked the poor girl what her dreams were."

"Bastard," Abby spit out.

If she hadn't spoken, Trinity would have forgotten she was there.

"There are a lot of them out there," Trinity replied.

"Speaking of assholes," Cade said. "There's a guy staying in the bunkhouse. He works for Lloyd. Thought you should know you won't be alone. Also, a ranch hand is arriving today. The only rule I have is don't sleep with anyone who works for me."

"We're back to that? If I wasn't certain you'd rescind your offer of a place to stay, I'd call you an asshole." She lifted her hands in question. "When do I get the benefit of the doubt? I never slept with anyone at McKinley Ranch. I learned from you, Dad, and Luke. Don't mix mattresses with money. I got it."

"I don't believe you. Men don't fight like that over nothing."

She laughed. It wasn't a feel-good laugh but an incredulous one. "So now I'm nothing?" She looked at Abby. "You want to know what happened? Here it is. For the men who'd been at the ranch forever, I was like a little sister or a daughter. No one bothered me. When Luke left, they replaced him with three guys because he is a Mosier, and we do the work of three men. Two of those men didn't like the word no, and they spread rumors about me. The way they told it, I was swinging from the rafters naked. The third guy didn't enjoy being left out, so he cornered me and meant to take what I hadn't offered. I punched him. Yes, there was a fight. Yes, it was about me, but not because I slept with all of them like they made everyone believe. It was because I wouldn't sleep with any of them."

She walked to the door. "I'll get settled in and look at your horses."

Cade stood and walked to stand beside her. "You probably should know—"

She held up a hand. "I've heard enough. My day is starting with a cloud hanging over my head, don't make it worse." She glanced past her brother. "Abby, thank you for everything."

"Anytime. Stop back for tea again soon."

Trinity opened the door, rushed out, and walked into a solid wall of chest. When she looked up, the cloud grew darker. Standing in her way was Tom Kincaid, the asshole who'd ruined everything in Wyoming.

"Unbelievable." She swung around to face her brother. "You hired this guy?" She raised her fisted hands in frustration, and Tom stepped back. "You might have snowed everyone that day, but I know the truth."

Tom smiled. "Hello, Trinity. Good to see you. Will we be sharing a bunk again?" He turned to Cade. "You said she wasn't around."

"She wasn't." Cade stepped between them. "And no one is sharing anything. If I hear about one fight, you're both gone."

Trinity stepped around her brother and pointed at Tom. "You stay away from me. I don't even want to breathe the air you do." She pointed to the bump on the ridge of his nose. "Does that still hurt after all these years?" She took a step forward, and Tom staggered back. "Probably not as much as your pride." She turned to

Cade. "You think I was trouble then? Just wait for this asshole to pull more of his shit."

"Trinity," Cade yelled. "You are here by a thread of my kindness."

She marched down the steps. "Don't give yourself that much credit. I'm here because Abby said I could stay."

CHAPTER SIX

Noise traveled in the valley between the two mountains. It was similar to yelling into a mason jar. There was no place for the sound waves to go, so they bounced back and forth.

Wyatt heard the commotion at Abby's as he threw his backpack into the front seat of this truck. Rather than ignore the problem, he drove straight toward it.

He didn't believe Cade's sister could be an issue. Most women were at most annoying. He had a sister and a mother, and the solution to all the problems they had was to listen and acknowledge. The voices got louder as he drew closer, and it was obvious someone wanted attention.

Standing on the porch was Cade. On each side of him, leaning toward one another like slathering dogs primed to attack, was a beautiful blonde and a cowboy he didn't recognize.

He threw his truck into park and rushed to help. By the look on the blonde's face, she was a tornado getting ready to spin, and if the hate in her eyes was any sign, she was capable of destruction.

"Trinity, calm down," Cade demanded.

So, this was the infamous Trinity. She was definitely a triple, as her name implied. She was tall, blonde, and gorgeous. She was also one pissed-off woman.

She stomped her boot and faced her brother. "Calm down? Have you ever walked into a hornet's nest?"

"Hey," Wyatt said. "Let's all take a step back." He moved between the cowboy and Cade's sister, turning his back to the man and looking straight into Trinity's eyes. They were a tempest on their own. He'd never seen eyes that were both land and sky, but hers started out brown at the iris and faded to a stormy blue at the edges.

To his relief, she stepped back and sucked in a big breath. "Who are you?"

He took her hand in his. "I'm Wyatt Morrison, and I think you need a change of scenery." He looked at the cowboy, whose sharp glare could slice a lesser man. Good thing for Wyatt he didn't flinch easily. "Can you ride a horse?"

She scoffed. "Can you pee standing up?"

He gently held her elbow and guided her down the steps. With a glance over his shoulder, he told Cade, "I'm kidnapping your sister for the day." He walked her to the truck. "You want some time in the saddle?"

"Is that a come-on? If so, I've heard it before."

"Nope. I've got two horses. One I favor and ride all the time, and one that could use some exercise." He opened the door and pointed inside the cab. "Looks like you need a cooling-off period."

"What I really need is a loaded gun or a branding iron

with the word idiot burning hot at the end." She climbed inside.

When he rounded the corner and sat behind the wheel, he turned to her. "You want to tell me what that was about?"

"Why, so you can report to my brother?"

He held his hands up in mock surrender. "Listen, I'm like Switzerland with your problems. I don't know you, and I barely know your brother, so there's no side for me to take."

She huddled against the door and blew out a breath. "That guy is the reason I had to leave my home and join the rodeo, which is just the Western version of the circus."

He chuckled. He'd never had a desire to take part in the rodeo. He was certain he could rope a steer or break a horse with the best of them, but those cowboys were human show ponies. They didn't get up with the sun and move cattle. Their horses weren't their best friends but a path to their next check. He didn't discount their commitment or their hard work, but it wasn't the same as being a rancher. That man on the porch she called an idiot was the real deal. All Wyatt had to see were his boots. They were scuffed and worn the way only a man who spent days on the range could beat up a pair.

"Relationship gone bad?"

"You'd think. You're just like everyone else who thinks my reputation is made on my back and not what I do in the saddle. I'm no buckle bunny."

"Never said you were." He put the truck in drive and kicked up a cloud of dust on their way out of town to the Big D Ranch. "Just trying to figure you out."

"Don't even bother. I won't be here long enough for it to matter."

"Fair enough."

"I can't believe Cade hired that asshole."

Wyatt lifted a brow. "Now you want to talk about it?"

"No, I don't."

"Is he competent?"

She shrugged. "With horses. I can't testify to any of his other skills."

He didn't miss her meaning.

"What about you? Tell me about your skills."

She twisted in her seat to face him. "Is this an interview?"

"Nope, just making sure you can handle Big Red."

"Is his name indicative of his temperament?"

Talk of horses appeared to interest her. She immediately sat up and leaned in.

"No, his coat. Although he's not patient with inexperienced riders. He needs someone to show him who's boss."

"I'll have no problem with him."

"Let's hope you're better with him than you are with the asshole at your brother's ranch."

They drove under the Big D sign onto the Dawsons' property.

"You've got to be kidding me." She twisted around to look at it from the backside. "Big D? What's wrong with men?"

"Women have been asking that same question for years. In this case, Lloyd Dawson owns the ranch."

"Oh, brother."

"Speaking of your brother, he considered naming his ranch the Big C."

What started as a giggle turned into a laugh. He

rather liked the sound of her laughter. He knew it would be better than facing her fury.

"I don't think there's a risk of that. Abby would kill him."

"I think you're right."

He parked his truck in front of the stables and tucked his keys into the glove box.

"What are we doing here?"

"This is where I work, and today you'll shadow me."

"You work here but live at Cade's. Why is that?"

"It's a long story that I don't have time to tell because I'm late. How are you with cattle?"

She opened the door. "You want me to ride them?"

He laughed. "No, we have to move them from one pasture to another. We'll have help. Baz and Lloyd will be there. Maybe Violet."

With any luck, Violet wouldn't be around. Her father had been most effective in keeping her away from him.

"I lived on a cattle ranch when I was a kid, but I remember very little."

He climbed out of the truck and hefted his backpack over his shoulder. "Same as riding a bike. It will all come back to you."

She followed him into the stables. "Only we're riding a horse." She immediately moved along the stalls and took in the horses.

He leaned against a support beam and watched her. Watching how they treated animals said a lot about a person. In his experience, most people treated animals better than they treated their fellow man. Horses had a sixth sense about people too. Red wasn't a fan of most humans, so his reaction to her would tell him something about Trinity.

"You must be Red." She stood a few feet from his stall and talked. "You are a big boy. Pretty too."

Wyatt moved closer to see if Red paid attention or gave her his ass end. It surprised him to watch the horse turn around and greet her.

"He's particular about his humans."

She turned toward him. "Can't blame him. Most aren't worth the time."

"Another cynic. You two will get along." He tapped a saddle draped over a wooden horse. "This is his."

She smiled, and it was like the light in the stable got brighter. "Nice to see he has his own saddle."

"He prefers it that way. I always thought sharing saddles was the equivalent of sharing underwear." He made a face. "Not a pretty thought. One size doesn't fit all." He stared in surprise as Red nuzzled into her hair, knocking off her hat. Wyatt bent to pick it up. "Can you have him saddled and fixed to go in fifteen?"

"Can a dog bark?"

As he readied Rex, he watched Trinity inspect the equipment before she took the horse from the stall. Her care of Red earned her bonus points. A cowboy was only as good as his horse.

Once saddled and ready to go, she walked him from the stable into the sun.

"You ready?" Wyatt asked when he moved next to her and climbed into Rex's saddle.

She tugged on the straps one more time. "I am."

"Need help to get up?"

Trinity cut him with a look that could wilt a flower. "Do you ask everyone who rides him that question or just me because I'm a girl?"

"I've never allowed anyone to ride him before."

47

Her eyes grew wide. "Why me?" She swung herself into the saddle and moved to Wyatt's side.

"Because it takes strength to weather a storm."

"Are you referring to me or the horse?"

He shook the reins and trotted forward. "Not sure yet."

They made their way to the southwest pasture labeled number four. Lloyd's ranch was large, and he moved his cattle frequently to keep the cows and the pasture healthy. Today they'd move a smaller herd from four to five.

Trinity rode beside him. Each time Red tried to show her he was boss, she reminded him of that error in thought.

"You're good with him."

"He's barely tolerating me. Maybe his name should be Cade."

"Remember, I'm Switzerland, but in your brother's defense, he's got a lot on his plate."

"If you're defending, you aren't neutral."

She had him there. "You're right." They neared the herd, and he saw Baz and Lloyd already rounding up the cattle to move them along. A person would think they'd be happy to go to a better restaurant where the food was plentiful, but each time the cattle got moved, it was a stampede. They acted as if Lloyd, Baz, and he led them off the side of a cliff. Then again, Lloyd raised them for slaughter. Yep, animals had a sixth sense.

"Who do we have here?" Lloyd asked.

Trinity thrust out her hand to shake his. "I'm Trinity Mosier, Cade's sister, and I hope you don't mind that I'm tagging along."

Lloyd glanced at Wyatt before a broad smile nearly

split his face. "You're with Wyatt?" Right then, Wyatt knew Trinity was the answer to his problems. "She is. Here with me, that is."

Baz nearly fell off his gelding. "No way. You can't possibly be Cade's sister. How old are you?"

She cocked her head, and Wyatt was certain she was considering something sinister. He moved his horse between them.

"Be careful with that one," he said to Trinity. "He likes older women."

She moved Red back to give him room. "How old is old?"

Baz ducked right and left until he got a clear view of her. "I'm not particular."

"Son, take your place."

"Fine." Baz moved off to the left of the herd. Lloyd galloped to the front.

"I'll take the right swing position. Lloyd has the point position, and Baz has the left. You can stick with me or take drag."

"What's drag?"

"You stay at the back and make sure the cattle don't turn. Red can help you figure it out. He's a natural. Or you can ride with me."

"I'll pull up the rear." She turned the horse and moved to the back.

"Same as riding a bike," he called after her.

"Never learned to ride one," she answered back.

Trinity Mosier was trouble, all right. How could he resist a woman who could tame his ornery horse with a touch and a word?

As they moved the cattle to their new home, he thought about her. She wasn't much different from the cows beside him. Prettier, but not all that dissimilar. If he read her right, all she wanted was a new pasture to settle down in.

Three hours later, after Baz took off and Lloyd left to meet a delivery of new steers, they were alone.

He slid from his saddle to the ground and tossed her a bottle of water he'd pulled from his saddlebag. "You hungry?"

"I am, but I'll survive. I didn't know this was an all-day field trip. I'm woefully unprepared." She uncapped the water and drank deeply.

"Come on down. I'm like a damn boy scout." He lifted a paper sack and pointed to a patch of ground beneath a large oak tree. Its leaves were new green and rustled in the wind. "Hope you like peanut butter and jelly." He tossed her a sandwich and took a seat.

She didn't scope out the grassiest area or lay down anything to cover the damp soil. She sank to the piece of land without a care to its comfort. Trinity was like no woman he knew.

"I'm impressed. You handled yourself well out there."

"It's not rocket science. I imagine it's harder to herd cats."

He took a bite of his sandwich. When he swallowed, he asked, "Have you ever tried to herd cats?"

"No, but I woke up to one in my face today."

He wasn't sure if he should make the joke that floated in his head. "I've got nothing to say to that."

She opened her sandwich to inspect the ingredients. "I bet you had a perfect response, but you're too nice to blurt it out. Every other guy would comment on how they would never complain about a 'kitty' in their face." She air-quoted kitty as if he didn't know exactly what she referred to.

"You've got me mistaken. I'm not that nice, and you're right. I don't know a man who would complain." He dug into his second sandwich. He always brought three. Today he'd do with less. "Something wrong with your sandwich?"

She took a bite and smiled. "Nope, it's one of the best things I've eaten this week."

"You need to up your culinary variety quotient. Maybe you should get closer to Baz. He's taking classes. That boy can make a mean brownie."

"I don't mind breaking in a new horse, but I have no interest in young boys. The fact he can cook is the most attractive thing about the kid."

"You can't cook?"

"I can hold my own."

"Great, I'd love to taste what you're offering."

She plucked the crust off her bread and tossed it toward a bird sitting on the fence. "I have nothing to offer, so you'll probably starve waiting on me."

He hopped to his feet. "I'll share anything I've got, so don't be afraid to ask." He offered his hand to help her up, and to his surprise, she took it. "You ready for more?" He loved how the double entendres filled the conversation with possibilities. Were they talking about cooking? Riding? It was open to interpretation. Cade described his sister as a tsunami. What would it be like to get caught up in her undertow?

They rode the fence for the next few hours and made their way back to the stables.

"Thank you for today. I needed it."

She took care of Red while he tended to Rex.

"There's nothing better for the soul than the outdoors," he said.

"Or a cheeseburger."

He chuckled. "There's that too." He walked inside Red's stall to make sure he had hay and water.

"Wyatt," Violet called from the stable door. "Are you in here?"

"Shit," he whispered.

The shuffle of Violet's boots neared. He needed to end her infatuation for good. He rushed to stand in front of Trinity. "Please don't hit me. Just play along." When Violet moved to the entrance of the stall, he cupped the back of Trinity's neck, knocking her hat to the ground. He pulled her toward him and crushed his lips against hers with more force than intended. She didn't fight him. She melted into him. Her hand went to his chest, and he expected a push, but it never came. She fisted the fabric of his shirt and yanked him closer.

Was it possible for her to enjoy the kiss? It wasn't something he planned, but a spur-of-the-moment reaction to Violet's visit. More shocking was when she opened her mouth. Who in their right mind wouldn't deepen the connection with a woman who was willing? One touch of her velvety tongue started a spark that raced through him. Unbridled desire galloped through his veins.

"Who the hell are you?" Violet screamed.

Trinity tapped at his chest like a wrestler who'd given up. When he backed off, she said, "I'm Trinity."

Wyatt pulled her to his side. "She's with me."

Violet turned the color of her name and stomped away.

"Who's Violet?" Trinity asked.

"The owner's daughter." He stepped back and licked his lips. "It's not what you think."

"It never is," she said.

"Thanks for saving me."

"I owed you one. Now we're even."

She bent to pick up her hat and walked from the stables acting like nothing had happened.

He found her sitting in the truck. Something told him they weren't even at all.

CHAPTER SEVEN

"What the hell was that?" she murmured.

Her lips tingled, and her heartbeat pounded in her ears. She told herself she didn't enjoy the kiss, that it was obvious Wyatt needed a rescue. He'd saved her that morning, so it was only right to pay him back.

She touched her kiss-swollen lips. Did she have to pretend to like it so much? Was she pretending? As soon as his hand cupped the back of her neck, she'd known what was coming. She melted into him like butter on a biscuit. Why him?

She shook her head. Vulnerability did a lot of things to a person, and in her case, it ended up making her needy for a touch of kindness. Now that it was out of her system, she could move on.

Her phone pinged, and she glanced at the screen.

Come to the main house.

A low garbled growl erupted from deep in her throat, and the fear of rejection escaped her heart and raced through her veins. Was Cade going to kick her out because of Tom? He'd had Cade's ear all day, and no doubt pleaded his case.

An unsettling laugh bubbled up. "He didn't need to plead his case," she said aloud. "All he needed to do was swing his—"

The door swung open, and Wyatt took a seat. "Are you ready?"

"Are you sure we don't have more fences to check?"

He chuckled. "We do, but that will take all day, and we'd get stuck in one of the weather shelters."

"You think Lloyd would rent me one?" she whispered.

"What was that?" He put the truck in gear and drove off the ranch.

"Nothing." She watched the valley turn into a forest. The pine trees stood tall next to each other like protective relatives. What would it feel like to have her family stand beside her? Would life have been different for her if she hadn't been born a girl?

"You bet it would," she blurted.

Wyatt glanced in her direction for a second. "What's that?"

"Nothing."

"That's a lot of nothing you're saying." He turned from the country road onto the highway.

She hadn't been here long enough to recognize any landmarks. It all looked the same.

"I have little to say."

She shifted ever so slightly to see the man next to her. She knew nothing about Wyatt except his last name, and that he was a competent cowboy and an excellent kisser.

"You want to talk about the kiss?" he asked.

"Not really." To discuss it would make it the nothing

it was. Keeping it to herself allowed her to pretend it was more. Wasn't it time she got a little more?

"I should apologize."

"You should, but don't. I get what it was."

He nodded. She wasn't in a chatty mood, and the more he pressed, the less she'd say.

"You hungry? We can stop by the diner to grab a bite if you'd like. I owe you at least that much."

She turned so her back was against the door. "My kisses are worth far more than a meal," she said.

"Understatement, but I wasn't talking about the kiss. I was referring to the work you did today. Having you pulling up the rear moved everything along quickly. Thank you for that."

"Thanks for the compliment, and for the offer. I'll have to pass." She lifted her phone into the air. "Cade has summoned me to the main house."

"Sounds ominous."

"I think it will be as pleasant as a splinter under my nail."

He drove down Main Street and pulled into a spot in front of the corner store. "I'll be right back. I need to pick up a few things." He hopped out of the truck and jogged into the store.

Trinity climbed out of the cab and glanced down the street. Aspen Cove was like all the other small towns she passed along the way. It had the basics and not much more. In fact, it might have less. There wasn't a bank or a bingo hall. She was also certain a good cup of coffee wouldn't exist anywhere.

It didn't matter. This was a stopover. The problem was she didn't know where the end destination would be. All she knew was she was here now.

Cade had told her to find a job. She looked down at her worn jeans and dusty boots. She had never interviewed for a position anywhere but was certain what she wore wouldn't impress. She needed something nicer. When her eyes lit on a sign that said dry goods, she smiled. Surely, they'd have clothes. Way back when, they called a country store a mercantile, and it would have sold everything from eggs to bolts of fabric. A modern dry goods store should have a shirt, and if she was lucky, underwear. At this point, she'd settle for the cotton white briefs grandmas wore. She perked up until she noticed the windows were whitewashed.

"You ready?" Wyatt placed his paper bag in the truck bed and took his seat.

She climbed in, and they were off.

"Where does a person buy clothes in this town?"

"They don't. I imagine Copper Creek or Silver Springs will have what you need."

"It's a possibility that I won't be here long enough to bother."

His jaw tightened. "Cade won't kick you out. You already made it past his flare-up and eruption."

"Cade is like Chernobyl. I may have avoided the worst of the disaster, but it's the fallout I fear." Her life was coated in the aftermath of other people's choices.

"You're safe. Abby seems on your side, and Cade isn't fond of sleeping in the trailer."

"Home sweet home," she said under her breath.

"What's that?"

"Nothing."

"It's always nothing with you." He pulled in front of Abby's cabin.

"Actually, it's always something with me if you listen to everyone else."

He hopped out and rushed around to open her door. "I'm not listening to anyone else. I'm listening to you."

"Shocker." She walked past him.

"Hey," he called as she made it onto the first step of the porch.

She spun around and held up her hand. "I know, don't tell anyone about the kiss."

His chin snapped back like she'd hit him. "No, that's not what I was going to say. While I rarely kiss and tell, I wouldn't presume to dictate how you should behave." He looked at the ground and kicked the dirt beneath him. "All I wanted to say was thanks for everything."

She gave him a weak smile. "You're welcome." She made it up another step before she turned to watch him round the truck. "Hey," she called out.

He stepped onto the running board and leaned over the roof. "Yeah?"

"I don't kiss and tell either. But Wyatt ... that kiss was worthy of a tell."

He laughed. "See ya, Three."

She cocked her head. "Three?"

He nodded. "Yep, you're blonde, bold, and definitely bad for me."

She stepped up one stair. "I'm more than that."

He chuckled and climbed inside.

She swore before the door closed, she heard him say, "God help me."

When she turned around, her brother stood leaning against the doorframe. "Come on in, and let's clear the air."

He didn't sound angry. Could she have misinterpreted his reason to want to see her? She was programmed to expect the worst, but maybe things were changing.

"Hi, Trinity," Abby said when she entered the house. "There's hot water on the stove. Tea and honey are on the table." She breezed past her. "I'm checking on the hives if you need anything." Abby walked out, closing the door behind her.

Trinity thought they were alone until she heard heavy footsteps come from the hallway. Tom strode out, zipping himself up.

She turned to her brother. "Really? How are we supposed to clear the air when you're polluting it with garbage?"

"Trinity. Stop." Cade pointed to the living room. It was a trait he'd learned from their father. When Trent Mosier snapped his fingers, everyone jumped, but Cade wasn't her daddy.

Instead, she moved into the kitchen and made a cup of tea. She picked the chamomile for its calming qualities but should have chosen the peppermint to settle her stomach. She drizzled honey from the dipper because she needed something sweet in her life.

She walked into the living room and sat on the stone hearth. It was the farthest she could get from Tom.

"Things being what they are," Cade started, "I thought it best to put you both in the same room and establish a set of rules."

Trinity didn't miss the lift of Tom's brows. He wasn't a man that paid much attention to rules, whether spoken or unspoken.

"I know the rules." She set her tea down and held up her palm like it was paper and moved across it with her finger like a pen. "Don't fight. Don't steal. Don't sleep with Cade's employees. Simple enough." She picked up her cup and took too big a drink. The hot liquid burned all the way down, but it wasn't nearly as painful as having to swallow her pride over and over again.

"Glad you figured it out," Tom snarled. He brought his hand to his nose.

She shook her head. "Oh, I figured you out a long time ago." She stood up and walked her empty teacup to the sink. "Too bad you could fool everyone else." She turned to her brother. "Watch this one. If you think I'm trouble, he's double. He pretends to know the rules, but he won't follow them. That guy there." She pointed to Tom. "He hates the word no."

Tom rose and marched toward her, so they were toe to toe. "No isn't a problem for me unless every other guy gets a yes."

"You two need to stop. If you can't get along, one of you will have to leave," Cade yelled.

Trinity pushed Tom out of the way. "We know who that will be." She walked toward the door.

"Come on, Trinity, that's not true. All I'm saying is I don't have the energy or the time for conflict. Get along." He looked from Tom to her. "Not worried about you two sleeping together since you can't stand to be in the same room. We all need something here." He glanced at Tom. "You need a job." He turned to Trinity. "You need a place to stay." He tapped his chest. "I need help."

"I can live with that," Tom said. He walked to where she stood by the door. "You do your thing, and I'll do mine."

She ignored him and leaned over to see her brother. "Are we finished?"

He nodded. "Are we clear?"

"As mud," she said and walked out.

She stomped across the field to the gate that separated Abby's property from Cade's. She had a choice. She could stay in the bunkhouse or the trailer. Wyatt and Tom would be in the cabin. Feeling her fist itch to punch Tom in the face again, she chose the trailer.

When she got there, she found a cold beer on the step. Beneath it was a note.

Not sure if you're staying in the trailer or the cabin. Thought I'd cover all bases. Not sure what's in there, but I know there isn't one of these. Let me know if you need anything else.

Wyatt

She uncapped the bottle on the conveniently located bottle opener attached to the side of the silver shoebox. "Designed by a man." She plopped herself down on the worn lounge chair. Her bottom fell through the spot where the plastic straps had given way. "Five-star experience." It wasn't the Ritz, but it was someplace, and that was always better than no place.

A cloud of dust rolled past her. When it settled, she watched Tom get out of his truck and walk toward the bunkhouse.

"Have a good night, Trinity." He tipped his hat as he walked inside the door.

"You too, asshole," she whispered, not loud enough for him to hear, but when he turned around to smirk, she flipped him the bird.

When she felt the strain of a full bladder, she rolled to her feet and entered the trailer. At five foot seven, she almost hit her head on the ceiling. She wondered how Cade had lived here. It was a tight, compact place. One end had a bed; the sheets were still crumpled from its last occupant—most likely Cade the night before.

There was a tiny sink but no running water. On the counter sat a single burner plugged into a solar battery pack. The panel leaned against the only window to eat up the light. A tiny refrigerator took up the under-cabinet space.

Her stomach grumbled, reminding her all she'd eaten was a part of a muffin and a peanut butter and jelly sandwich. She opened the fridge and found nothing but a slice of moldy cheese. On the countertop was an open box of crackers.

After a cup of tea and a beer, her bladder screamed for relief. She turned around and saw the bathroom. There was one door, and when she opened it, she wanted to cry. Inside was a composting toilet that looked new and unused. From the ceiling, dropped the showerhead.

"All in one."

When her jeans were at her knees, she stopped. Using the toilet meant she'd have to empty it, and that wasn't happening. Her life had enough crap in it as it was; she didn't need to add additional nastiness to the mix. If Cade hadn't used it, there was a reason. Her brother could be an asshat, but he was rarely an idiot.

She yanked up her jeans. Wyatt said to tell him if she needed anything, and she had to pee. She hopped down the two steps to the ground and raced toward the bunkhouse.

CHAPTER EIGHT

Having a bunkmate would take some getting used to. Wyatt had grown accustomed to peaceful evenings, but as soon as Tom stomped inside grumbling about women being worthless, he knew his life would change.

"There are two rooms that are open. Choose the one that suits you best." Wyatt stood in the kitchen, forming hamburger patties. Trinity's mention of them earlier had created a craving. He didn't know why he called her Three. It wasn't his usual practice to give anyone a nickname, but it felt right with her.

Tom plopped into the corner chair. "Where's the television?"

"We don't have one." He put the burgers in the skillet and washed up.

"What's for dinner?"

"I'm having burgers. Not sure what you're having. What did you bring to eat?"

A knock sounded. Wyatt dried his hands and threw the worn towel over his shoulder on the way to the door.

When he opened it, there stood Trinity. "Hey, Three. Long time no see."

"Umm, can I use the bathroom?" She looked over her shoulder to the trailer. "The amenities are scarce. The toilet is basically a litter box."

Tom leaned forward. "Go piss in the bushes like the rest of us. You're not welcome in here."

Wyatt pinched the bridge of his nose; he didn't need this shit. Life was complicated enough. There was no room for childish behavior.

"Grow up. She has as much right to be here as you or me." He stepped aside and pointed to his right. "First door on the left."

She ran down the hallway.

"I don't want her here," Tom said.

"You don't have a choice. She's Cade's sister."

"He probably doesn't want her here either."

Wyatt went back to his burgers and flipped them. "She's here, so live with it." He sprinkled on garlic powder, salt, and pepper. "Didn't your mom teach you to respect women?"

Tom laughed. "Man, you've got it all wrong. Trinity isn't a woman. Look past the long blonde hair and tits, and she's a man with a vagina."

She walked down the hallway. "Or a girl with a dick. One bigger than yours." She lifted her nose and breathed deep. "Smells good."

Wyatt leaned on the counter and looked at her. "You hungry?"

Tom jumped to his feet. "Whoa, you told me to get my own, but you'll feed her?"

Wyatt opened two buns and handed a plate with one to Three. "She's proven her worth. You haven't shown me shit but a bad attitude." He flipped the burgers once more and set one on top of each bun. "I don't have the fancy stuff, but there's ketchup and mustard in the fridge."

She covered the patty with the other bun. "I'm easy."

"Got that right," Tom said.

This wasn't Wyatt's ranch. If it was, he'd take Tom out and show him some manners. He walked to the table, set his plate down, and pulled a chair out for Three. He took his seat because if he didn't, Tom would get a beat down.

"Let's establish some rules. We all live here. There won't be any fighting. If you can't be nice, then get the hell out." He took a bite of his burger.

"Who made you king?"

Wyatt took the edge of the towel that hung over his shoulder and wiped the juice running down his chin. "Squatter's rights. I've been here longer than you. I set this place up. You have a problem with me, then go talk to Cade. If you're hungry, there's a can of stew in the cupboard, or if you hurry, the diner is still open."

Three stood up and turned in the direction of Tom. "You ready to call it a truce?"

Tom eyed her. "We ain't friends, Trinity."

"Nope, but we're neighbors. You stay out of my way, and I'll keep out of yours."

Tom walked out the front door. Seconds later, his engine started, and he left.

"I don't want to cause trouble, Wyatt." Three nibbled around the edge of her burger.

"If the rumors are true, that's your superpower."

She shook her head. "Don't believe everything you hear."

"I never do." He leaned over to grab a bag of chips sitting on the counter. "You want some?"

She nodded. "More than you know."

They ate in companionable silence. When she finished, she rose and started tidying up.

"I don't expect you to clean."

"I know. I'm doing it because you didn't expect it. If you did, I wouldn't have lifted a finger."

He sat back and watched her clean the kitchen area. "Are you always so contrary?"

She turned off the water and set the frying pan on the counter to dry. "Sometimes, I'm worse."

He went to the fridge and pulled out another beer. "You want one?"

"I didn't come over to eat your food and drink your beer."

He twisted the cap and handed the bottle to her. "No, you came to pee." He took a long draw and nodded to the door. "How about a walk?"

She followed him outside. "Are you ready to discuss the girl in the barn?"

"Nothing to talk about. She's a girl who thinks I'm the one, but I'm not. What about you? You want to tell me why you and Tom hate each other?"

He led her to the pond where they took a seat on the big rock. A sparkling blanket of stars covered the sky.

She laid back and stared upward. "Nope, Cade doesn't care. Why should you?"

"I'm not Cade."

"Thank goodness for that. I love my big brother, but sometimes he's as stubborn as a mule."

She pushed up and sat with her feet dangling over the edge.

"Sounds like a family trait."

She looked away. "What Tom said ... it wasn't untrue." She picked up a pebble and tossed it into the water. A ripple moved across the surface. Not one part was unaffected. That was the thing about change. It created a disturbance, and when something interrupted the calm, it would never be exactly the same again.

"What part?" His mind ran through the evening. There was a lot said. It wasn't the words he heard but the actions he saw. Tom was dead set on hurting Three.

"I was raised on ranches to be one of the boys. I've lived in bunkhouses my entire life."

The wind whipped around them, and her hair blew across her face. He reached out to brush it aside. "You are not like any guy I know, but after meeting Tom, I'm sure you beat him in the endowment department."

She laughed. "I wouldn't know. I've never seen his. Contrary to popular belief, I'm not easy."

He immediately felt guilty for kissing her that afternoon. In what world was it okay to grab an unsuspecting woman and lay his lips on her? "Trinity, I'm so sorry for this afternoon. I didn't understand how that might make you feel. I was selfish and inconsiderate."

She turned to look at him—stare at him as if she was analyzing his intentions. "I like when you call me Three."

He stood and offered his hand. "Well, Three, I'm sorry for being an asshole."

She pulled herself up and stood beside him, looking at the water. "You're better than most." She tapped her chest. "I feel it in my heart." She looked toward Abby's house. Under the light of the moon, she smiled. "Don't tell him I have one."

"Your secret is safe with me." He helped her off the

rock, and they walked back toward the trailer. "Get your stuff. I'll show you your room."

"I'll stay here."

"Not a chance. I lock the door at night, which means you have to knock to use the bathroom." He rubbed his hand over his face. "I need my beauty sleep."

"You lock the door? Are you afraid someone will break in and kill you?"

He chuckled. "Kind of. I'm afraid Violet will sneak in, and Lloyd will kill me."

She stopped and turned toward him. "Basically, you need me as your shield."

He rocked his head back and forth. "And I'll act as yours. Now get your stuff. It's dark, I'm tired, and my mattress is calling me."

She rushed into the trailer and came out with a backpack and a purse. "This is all I've got."

Three was a puzzle to him. She was as pretty as a princess and as tough as a soldier. She rode a horse like a wrangler but had the softness of a kitten.

"You want help with your luggage?" he teased.

She tossed him her purse. "Yeah, you take the heavy one."

They walked into the cabin. It didn't have much to offer. There were a few chairs, an old sofa, and a card table where they ate. For all intents and purposes, it was drab and dreary, but Three brightened up the place with her presence. She was a single rose in a glass vase. Alone. Pretty. Fragrant. Thorny. Delicate. She would wither if not cared for. Something inside Wyatt wanted that job.

He passed the room he bunked in and turned into the second one. Not seeing any of Tom's things, he set her purse on the dresser. He'd been collecting donations to furnish the place for weeks. There were two beds and two dressers in each room. Nothing matched, but it didn't have to. Most were happy to have a place to call home.

"I think Abby put sheets and towels in the drawers." He turned to leave. At the door, he pointed to the lock. "Use it. I don't want Tom bothering you."

She laughed. "The last time he did, I broke his nose."

He held back his smile. "Good night, Three."

"Night, Wyatt." As the door was about to click shut, she said, "I didn't really mind the kiss."

Neither did I. He walked into the room next to hers and stripped down for bed. Three would be trouble all right. He had a weakness for women who were funny, feisty, and fabulous.

CHAPTER NINE

Trinity knew she'd slept in. She felt it in the way her muscles dragged when she climbed out of bed. There was no need to look at her phone for the time. The silence of the house told her everything. Half the workday was over.

She grabbed her towel, tossed her bag over her shoulder, and peeked out the door to make sure no one was skulking about before she rushed to the bathroom in her bra and underwear.

She leaned over the sink to look in the mirror. Dark circles rested under her eyes.

"You're a mess, girl," she said to herself.

She stripped out of her undergarments and climbed in the shower. It wasn't luxurious, but it was wet and remarkably clean. With Tom around, that would change. He wasn't a details kind of guy. She hoped her brother had gotten him cheap.

She lathered up and rinsed, then wet her hair and glanced around for the shampoo but found none. "That's right. They're heathens." Her hair would hate her, but a girl had to go with the flow, so she used the bar soap.

When she finished, she stepped out, ready to conquer the day.

Cade had told her to find a job. Abby said she could care for the horses. The latter would feed her; the former might get her some shampoo and a change of underwear.

In the kitchen, an old coffeepot sat on the counter. At the bottom was an inch of caffeinated mud, just the way she liked it; coffee, she could almost chew. She downed it and headed for her SUV and a trip into town.

She parked in front of the pharmacy. She had priorities. Shampoo, conditioner, and toilet paper that didn't sand her bottom were at the top of the list.

The bell above the door rang when she stepped inside. Behind the counter stood a white-haired woman with kind eyes and a welcoming smile.

"Mornin'," she said. "Welcome to Doc's. I'm Agatha."

"Good morning." She reached for her hat to take it off out of courtesy but remembered she'd left it at the cabin. "I'm Trinity."

Agatha closed the paper and leaned on the surface. "You new in town or just visiting?"

"Not sure yet. I'm Trinity. Cade and Luke's sister."

"I know your brothers. That Luke is something else. His girl Riley makes these big metal pieces people pay thousands for. Cade sticks to himself, but he makes our Abby happy so that makes us happy."

"Good to know." She moved toward the counter and snatched up a chocolate bar. "Where would I find shampoo?"

"Let me think." She put her finger to her chin and looked up. "It's in the cleaning supply aisle. Three down to your right. Paul has a system that only makes sense to him."

Trinity thought the woman had lost her mind, but when she turned down the aisle, she found the shampoo sitting beside the dishwashing detergent, which was stored next to the granite cleaner. In some crazy way, she got his system.

Not wanting to bother the older woman, she considered where the conditioner might be. It was a kind of lotion for the hair. She located it sitting next to a bottle of Nivea. Looking for the toilet paper was easy. It was with everything else made to absorb, like sponges and mops and tampons.

Back at the counter, she set her selections down and took out her wallet. There wasn't much in there. Gas had eaten her resources to get here. Inside was the check from Blain and not much more.

Agatha rang up her purchases. "That will be nine sixty-one."

Trinity moved the chocolate bar into view. "Did you get this too?"

Agatha added it to the bill. "That's ten eighty-five."

She had a five, four ones and some change. She'd need to find a bank soon.

"Can I put this back?" She held up the candy bar.

Agatha stared at her with soft, mothering eyes. Not that she knew how a mother looked at their child, but if she'd had a mom, she was certain the expression would be similar.

"Is this your first trip to town?"

"Yes. Well, I mean, I was here yesterday with Wyatt, but I stayed outside while he ran into the corner store."

Agatha bagged the goods. "First ten bucks is on us."

"Really?"

The older woman's cheeks turned pink. "It builds

goodwill and ..." She paused like she was making it up on the fly. Trinity wasn't sure she wasn't. "That brings you back."

She handed Agatha a dollar. "My bill was over ten."

"Close enough." She thrust the bag forward. "I look forward to seeing you again, Trinity."

"I'll definitely be back. Do you know anyone who's hiring?"

Agatha smiled. "Check the bakery or the brewhouse. Maisey's might need a little help too until Natalie gets back."

"I will." She walked out of the pharmacy and into the sun. The golden rays caressed her cheeks. Across the street was the bakery. Down the road was the fire station. She debated on which to visit first. The bakery where she might get a job or the firehouse where she would find the nice brother. When her stomach grumbled, she dropped her bag at her SUV and headed straight toward the smell of chocolate.

She entered heaven and glanced at the offerings in the glass case.

"Howdy," a blonde from behind the counter popped up and said. Her Texas drawl was a reminder to Trinity of the years she'd spent in Dallas.

"Howdy back. The chocolate roped me in."

"That would be the muffins." The woman reached over and offered a hand to shake. "I'm Katie, and you are?"

She gave her a firm shake and dropped her hand. "I'm Trinity Mosier."

"As in Luke and Cade?"

She raised her hands in the air in mock surrender. "Guilty."

"When did you get here?"

She moved sideways to take in everything. There were cookies and cakes and muffins and something that looked like a brownie covered in caramel and nuts.

"I arrived the day before yesterday. I'm staying at Cade's ranch for now."

Katie pointed to a table under a corkboard labeled as the Wishing Wall. "Have a seat. First treat is on the house. You like chocolate?"

"I like everything." *But raisins.* She didn't admit that because it wasn't nice to criticize.

Katie giggled. "My kind of girl."

Trinity sat at the designated table and looked up to the board. There were notes pinned in various places. Some were serious, asking for healing. Some were silly, asking for first kisses.

Katie sat a plate in front of her. "Coffee or milk?" She had both balanced in one palm.

"Coffee, please."

"Perfect, I'll drink the milk." She took a seat. "That's the Wishing Wall. You want to fill one out?"

Trinity shook her head. "I don't really believe in wishes. I believe in hard work."

"It's possible to believe in both."

Trinity stared at the plate full of treats. "Are we having a party? Who will eat all of this?"

"Take home what you don't eat." She pulled open the carton and drank deep. "Tell me what brings you here."

They sat together like they were friends. Trinity had never had a female friend. There weren't many women on the ranches where she'd worked. The ones that showed up were gone by first light.

She wasn't sure how this sharing thing went. Did she tell her everything or spoon-feed her the basics? Too much of anything was never good, so she shared only a bit.

"I lost my job in Dallas and came here to regroup."

Katie smiled. "I'm from Dallas. Where did you work?"

That Southern twang made Trinity feel at home. She'd been hearing it for years.

"I trained horses for Blain Wallaby."

Katie lifted a brow. "Oh my. How was that?"

"Fine, until he fired me."

"Let me guess, new trainer for his Angel?"

Trinity stared, slack-jawed. "You know them?"

"They're the Wallabys. Big money, little brains. I mean really, who has a ranch named Wallaby but raises horses?"

"Mr. Wallaby, I guess." She pulled off the top of the muffin and took a bite. "Oh, my goodness. This is ..."

"Heaven, right? When Bea died, she left all her recipes. You'd think there was magic in them, but it's mixing the right stuff together that makes it good. Don't worry about Blain; he wasn't the best ingredient for you. I imagine you'll find everything you need right here in Aspen Cove."

"What I really need is a change of clothes." She pointed to herself. "This is all I got. I washed my underwear in the sink, and they're hanging from the knob of my dresser to dry. Probably too much information but Agatha told me to come here. Said you might know of someone who's hiring."

Katie rubbed her chin. "Go see Cannon at the brewhouse. I think he might need someone." She giggled like

75

she had a secret. "As for clothes, what size are you? A six?"

Trinity shook her head. "No way. I live on burgers and junk food. I'm tall, so I look thinner, but I'm a solid ten. After this plate of sweets, maybe a twelve."

Katie took a sticky note off the wall and put it and a pen in front of Trinity. "Humor me. Write your wish. It can't hurt."

Trinity scribbled the words *a change of clothes* on the note and tacked it to the board. "Done." She finished her muffin and drank the watered-down coffee before she stood. "I'll take the rest with me." She figured Wyatt might enjoy the brownie, or maybe Abby would like the cookie.

Katie jumped up and rushed around the counter, coming back with a bag and a box. "Will you be seeing Luke?"

"He's next on my list."

"Perfect. Can you bring this to him?" She lifted the box. "He loves Wednesday's chocolate chip muffins."

She bagged up the leftovers and tucked the box under her arm. Goodbyes were always awkward. She didn't know if she should wave, walk away, or shake Katie's hand. With guys, it was easy. All they did was get up, nod their heads, and walk off. This experience was new.

Katie didn't give her a chance to wonder too long. She opened her arms and tugged Trinity in for a hug. "You stop by anytime, and don't forget to ask Cannon about a job."

When Katie let her loose, Trinity walked to the door. "Is this town for real?"

The trill of Katie's laughter filled the bakery. "Almost spooky, right? But don't worry, you'll fit right in. You belong to Luke and Cade, which means you're family to all of us."

Trinity walked out, feeling like she was dreaming and moved down the sidewalk carrying a box of muffins for her brother. She turned into the fire station to find four men winding hoses. Two stopped dead and stared at her.

Luke tugged on the hose, and when he realized the others had dropped their sections, he lifted his chin.

"Trin? Is that you?"

She waited for him to point his finger to the exit and yell "Out," but he didn't. He rushed over and wrapped her in a hug. *Maybe I picked the wrong brother's doorstep to land on.*

"Introductions please," said one of the younger men in his station.

Luke scowled. "James, Jacob." He pointed to the door. "Out."

"Geez, man, you can't have all the pretty girls."

"This is my sister Trinity, and she's off-limits."

The two younger men frowned at each other and walked away.

Trinity realized she still had the box of muffins. "Katie sent these over."

He took the box and showed her to his office. "Have a seat. You didn't tell me you were coming."

She sat in the chair in front of his desk. "I figured, better to beg for forgiveness than ask for permission."

"How long are you staying?" He leaned in and breathed in the baked goods.

"You sharing?" the fourth man from the garage said. He didn't wait for an answer but entered and took a muffin.

"This is Thomas," Luke said.

Trinity lifted from the chair. "Pleased to meet you, Thomas. I'm Trinity."

"My pleasure meeting you, too." He looked at Luke. "You mind if I sneak out to see Eden and the baby?"

Luke nodded toward the door, "Tell them hello."

"Are you staying in Aspen Cove?" Luke tilted his head.

"Are you worried?"

He waved her off. "You were never a problem for me." He took a bite of the muffin and set it down. "I'd offer our place, but we don't have a room for you. Riley has the spare space turned into a workshop."

"I'm sleeping in the bunkhouse at Cade's. He's not happy, but he's letting me stay until I find something else."

"Good. I could ask around and see if anyone has a place for rent."

"Let me find a job first, and I'll let you know. I've got a lead on something." She stood. "In fact, I should be going."

"It's good to see you, Trin. You need to come by and have dinner or something. Or at least go to the diner sometime to meet Riley."

"That sounds great." She left and made her way down the street toward Bishop's Brewhouse. She took a deep breath and said a silent prayer before she walked inside.

"You must be Trinity," the man behind the counter said. "Can you start tomorrow night?"

She moved toward the bar. "Are you Cannon?"

"Yep, and I need someone to wait tables a few days a week."

"You don't want to interview me?"

"I don't need to. Katie said you were nice."

She leaned against the wooden counter, fearing her knees would buckle. Was she more afraid of working at something other than horses or failing?

"I've never worked with anything but horses."

"You can't be any worse than Goldie was when she started. She hadn't worked with anything beyond makeup and fancy clothes. You'll feel right at home because many of my customers can be a horse's ass."

"That's it? I show up and work? Is there something I need to wear?"

He shook his head. "Clothes." He filled up bowls with pub mix and set them on the bar. "You can fill out your paperwork tomorrow. See you at five."

She left the brewhouse feeling dazed. Being in Aspen Cove was equal to entering an episode of the *Twilight Zone*.

She sat in her SUV and searched for a nearby Chase Bank. There was one in Copper Creek. On her way out of town, she stopped at the gas station. A woman walked out and waved.

Trinity spent the last of her cash on gas. She was almost surprised the woman didn't rush over and tell her it was free. Relieved actually, because, in her experience, every gift needed repayment, and she was cash broke, and emotionally empty.

After pumping, she walked inside the station and put her nine dollars on the counter.

"You must be Trinity. I'm Louise."

"News travels fast."

She nodded. "Good news for sure." She took the money and stuck it in the register. "I would have given you the gas, but I've got eight kids." She pointed to the rack of chips and jerky. "Take a snack as our welcome gift."

"Eight kids? Wow."

Louise blushed. "I know. It's a lot, but I wouldn't send one of them back." Louise gathered a few things from the display. "Take these and come back and see us."

Trinity shook her head. "I wasn't expecting anything."

"It's the unexpected that brings us the most joy." She pushed the chips and jerky into Trinity's hands.

"I'm not sure I can handle anything else. I'm on kindness overload."

"Well, hold on because your ride has just begun."

Trinity didn't know how to interpret that. Did she know about the ranch and the trouble she had with Cade? Not knowing how to respond, she smiled, waved, and walked away.

Copper Creek was a fail except for depositing her check. Since it came from out of state and was drawn on a different bank, they would hold the funds until they cleared. Her dream of stopping at Target to get underwear and a change of clothes would have to wait. The only good part was the teller gave her a sucker and showed her how to use the online app.

When she pulled in front of the bunkhouse, Tom was standing on the porch. He held a bag in his hands.

"Someone named Katie dropped this off for you."

Trinity saw the bag overflowing with clothes.

"Wow, everyone is so nice here." She wanted to amend that to exclude him, but she behaved.

He shoved the bag into her arms. "Well, they don't know you yet."

CHAPTER TEN

"Where's your girlfriend?" Violet asked.

Her comment stumped Wyatt for a second. He didn't have a girlfriend.

"You mean Three?"

She frowned. "Isn't her name Trinity?"

"I call her Three. I mean, that is what the trinity is, anyway. Only she isn't celestial." *That kiss I stole from her was.*

Violet let her petulant teen come out. "Whatever," she said with a roll of her eyes. "Why isn't she here?"

He stored his saddle and picked up his backpack. He hadn't seen Trinity since the night before last when they'd shared a burger and a beer.

He knew she was in the bunkhouse because her shampoo filled the air. The place smelled like tropical fruit instead of damp wood. He passed by her closed door several times but figured if she was in a social mood, she would have come out to visit.

"She's at home." He didn't know for certain, but it was a safe answer. "I'm out of here." It had been a long day on the range. Three calves had been born with one needing assistance. Nothing like being up to his elbow inside a cow to help pull out her calf.

He didn't wait for Violet's response. He moved past her to his truck. He made the drive back to Cade's on autopilot. When he arrived at the bunkhouse, Trinity's white SUV was nowhere in sight.

Walking back from the barn were Cade and Tom. The latter moved past him with no acknowledgment. Cade stopped to say hello.

"How did the day go at Big D?"

Wyatt leaned against the rail of the porch. "Three calves born today. I suspect we'll have more tomorrow." He looked down at his dirty clothes. "I really need a shower then a beer in that order."

"A beer sounds good."

"Where's your sister?"

Cade glanced over his shoulder like he hadn't noticed her SUV missing.

"She got a job."

Wyatt's eyes grew wide. "Really? That was fast. I thought she'd be helping you around the ranch."

"Having Trinity work with Tom would be like putting two rabid dogs into a single kennel."

He wasn't sure he had a right to say anything, but Cade didn't give his sister enough credit. He'd seen trouble in his life, and Three wasn't the poster child.

"I'm not sure she's the problem." He nodded to the door. "Is that guy trustworthy? I mean, he was incredibly rude to your sister the other night. If I hadn't been there, she would have had to piss in the bushes."

"She's staying in the bunkhouse?" He rubbed at his chin. "I thought she'd stay in the trailer."

"That was her plan, but the amenities are lacking. I convinced her to take a room."

"You might regret that." He looked toward Abby's cabin. "If you want a beer, I've got cold ones at the house. Come on over once you're showered."

Wyatt pushed off the rail. "How about a trip to the brewhouse? I love the amber ale they have on tap."

Cade groaned. "That place is off-limits to me. That's where my sister got a job." He shook his head. "First, she got me kicked out of my house, and now she's infiltrated the watering hole."

That piece of information made Wyatt smile. "You don't give her enough credit. Or ... maybe you give her too much. Have you ever considered her behavior is a response to others?"

"Look, I know her. She's too pretty for her own good. Men love her. Women hate her. She may not cause the problem, but she's always at the center."

"Seems unfair."

Cade kicked at the dirt beneath his boots. "Life isn't fair." He took a step toward home. "Beers are cold if you want one."

Bishop's Brewhouse sounded tempting before he knew Three worked there, but now it was more appealing. He could honestly say hamburgers and a beer with her were the highlight to his week. And that kiss. It might have been the best one of his life. If men fought over her, it was because she had something they wanted.

When he entered the bunkhouse, Tom stood dripping wet and wearing a towel in the kitchen. He threw two pieces of bologna on white bread.

"I'd offer you dinner, but sharing doesn't seem to be a thing here."

"Thanks, but I'm heading out. I don't mind sharing, but I do mind assholes. Until you stop being one, I'm not interested in anything you offer."

Tom walked over to the worn leather chair in the corner and plopped down. "You're after what Trinity offers, and I'm telling you, man, you don't want that. She passes out favors like penny candy on Halloween."

Wyatt desperately wanted to defend her honor, but he didn't know the truth. Three didn't seem like a woman who was indiscriminate about lovers. He refused to take the advice of a guy who thought two slices of bologna and two pieces of bread counted as dinner.

"Something tells me you were a trick-or-treater at her door, and she gave you nothing."

Tom kicked off the chair and stomped past him to the hallway. When he got to his door, he said, "What do you know?"

Wyatt walked to his room. "Not a damn thing, but I want to know everything."

Twenty minutes later, he drove off the ranch toward town. He found a parking spot in front and walked inside. Behind the counter was Trinity, looking all flustered. Next to her was Goldie.

He moseyed to the bar and took a seat.

"I'll be right with you," Three said without looking up. "What am I doing wrong to get so much head on the beer?"

Goldie laughed. "It's the angle of the mug when you pour."

Wyatt watched Goldie fill a perfect mug. "You try."

Three looked up and noticed him. "Oh, it's you."

"Is that good or bad?"

"Good. I needed a friendly face." She shook her head

and smiled. "Who knew that giving a guy too much head was a bad thing?"

"Only for beer," he said. "I'll take an amber ale."

She pulled out a frosted mug and tipped it under the spigot, but her geometry skills were off, and the beer hit the bottom, then sloshed out onto her T-shirt. How the cotton stuck to her stomach told him it wasn't the first time it happened.

"I'm cursed."

Goldie patted her on the back. "You practice on Wyatt, and I'll get the boys at the pool table."

He turned to see who was playing. Dalton's friends were back. They weren't the only ones in the bar. With the growth in Aspen Cove, several construction crews came and went. He didn't recognize the rowdy guys in the corner.

"How was work?" Three asked. "Any problems with your admirer?"

"Besides being pissy because I have a girlfriend?"

She finished the pour and slid it to him. There were five inches of beer and two of foam. It was a good start.

"Now I'm your girlfriend?"

He sipped his beer. "I bought you dinner."

"I'm not that cheap or easy."

He nodded. "Something tells me that's true."

The guys in the corner raised their glasses, and Three groaned. "Looks like I'm up."

She rounded the bar with a tray and trudged toward them.

Wyatt pivoted on the chair to watch. She approached them but didn't get too close. One man reached out and pulled her by the belt loop, tugging her into his lap. He would have pinned her there if Three wasn't so quick to free herself.

Wyatt made to get up but thought better of it. Sometimes it was better to observe than to act. She had lived in bunkhouses all her life. He was interested to see how she handled the men.

One guy placed his hand on her bottom. If Tom and Cade were right, he assumed she'd giggle and smile. Maybe she'd flirt to get the extra tip, but not Three. She bent over and whispered something into his ear, and the guy dropped his hand and shifted away.

Once she had their orders, she swung around and returned to the taps. "What a bunch of idiots." She put four frosted mugs on the counter and set out to fill them up. "It's a wonder we evolved past pounding chests, pulling hair, and caves. I'm tempted to bring them a box of matches and show them fire for the first time."

He loved her sassy mouth.

"You seemed to handle it all right. What did you tell the groper?"

She finished pouring the first mug and moved on to the second. "I told him you were my boyfriend, and you had a concealed carry." She winked. "Said the 45 in your boot was itching to come out and play."

He laughed. "Really?"

She shook her head. "No, that would have been too many words to string together for him to understand."

"What did you tell him?"

She set the second mug on the tray.

She smiled. He knew why men fought over her. It was the chance to make her luscious lips tip up. "I told him I worked on a cattle ranch castrating bulls, and if he didn't keep his hands to himself, he'd be next."

He squirmed on his seat. "That would do it."

She filled the rest of the mugs up and took them straight to the table. This time no one touched her, but Wyatt could see they wanted to.

There was nothing provocative about the way she dressed. Baggy jeans and a T-shirt, that came high on her neck, didn't shout party girl or tramp. Her face was makeup free, and her hair was pulled into a ponytail. She was beautiful. Maybe Trinity was the perfect name because she was otherworldly.

When she returned, she leaned on the bar and sighed. "I'm in hell."

"If you hate this job so much, why do it?"

"Because I like to eat, and it would be amazing to have a change of underwear." She pointed to her outfit. "These showed up on the porch yesterday. This town is really something. However, the owner was shorter than me. The hem sits on my shins. Thank God for boots." She lifted one foot to show him the denim tucked inside.

"Someone brought you clothes? Who?"

She lifted her shoulders. "Not sure, but I'm guessing Katie. I put a wish on the board, and by the time I got back to the bunkhouse, there was a bag of clothes waiting." She leaned in, so their noses nearly touched. "The pharmacy gave me shampoo and conditioner, and Katie gave me treats. Speaking of which, I've got half a brownie in my room for you."

He lifted a brow. "Only half?"

Her cheeks turned pink. "I got hungry and ate part, but if you stop by when I get home, I'll give you your half." "You could have eaten anything that's mine. I don't want you starving."

She stood and waved him off. "I don't like to owe

anyone." She patted her back end. "It's not like I'll starve to death."

"Seriously, Three. You need to eat. A girl can't live off half a brownie."

She smiled. "Oh, I didn't. I ate the cookie I brought home for Abby too." She reached into the pub mix jar and popped a few crackers into her mouth. "These are tasty as well."

"We'll talk about that later." He checked his watch. "You hungry now?" If he hurried, he could get something at the diner before it closed.

"I'm good." She looked toward the corner where the rowdies sat holding their empties in the air.

"I'll be right back." Wyatt slid off his chair and walked out the door. As he passed the men in the corner, he gave them a look that said, *don't mess with my girl.*

He laughed all the way to the diner. What in the world made him think of Three as his? Maybe it was because Tom was such a jerk or because Cade hadn't shed a flattering light on his sister. Everyone needed someone to back them up. How long had it been since Trinity had a champion in her corner?

He stepped inside Maisey's. Riley rushed over. "We're closing in ten."

"What do you have that's quick and easy?"

"I've got a Salisbury steak blue plate special. I think there's a few left."

"I'll take two and a piece of pie."

"Two? You got a date?"

"Nah, just feeding Three."

She cocked her head. "You need three?"

He pulled out his wallet. "No, it's for Trinity and me. She's working at the brewhouse and hasn't eaten."

Riley fisted her hips. "Why didn't she tell me?" She pointed to a table by the window. "She sat right there with Luke and drank a glass of water but said nothing about not eating."

"Pride, probably."

"No place for that in Aspen Cove. Give me a few minutes, and I'll have your order ready."

He pulled twenty-five dollars from his wallet. "Here you go."

She shook her head. "I'm not taking your money to feed Trinity. She's family."

"Well, I'm not family, and I'd like to pay for both."

"You know the saying, want in one hand and spit in the other and see what fills up faster."

"I don't think it's spit."

Riley turned and disappeared into the kitchen. Within minutes she was back with two Styrofoam containers.

"Thanks for looking out after her." She chewed on her lip. "Luke said she's had a tough life."

That was probably an understatement. "Thanks for the food." He backed toward the door. "I'll take care of her."

He was only outside a second when the open sign in the window turned off, and Riley clicked the door locked. Back in the brewhouse, he took his seat at the bar.

Three was back at the table with the men who looked like they'd had one too many already. She slapped the tab on the table and told them she couldn't serve them another round.

One guy tried to tuck a twenty into her shirt. She pushed his hand away. Three wasn't anything like Tom described. He'd seen his fair share of women who manipulated men to get what they wanted. Any girl would have gladly taken the money and run. Three needed the job. She was desperate for money, but she wasn't willing to lower her standards to get it.

"That went over like a pregnant pole vaulter," she said.

"That's a vision I don't want to imagine."

She laughed.

Goldie moved behind the bar and began to wash glasses. "What's so funny?"

"Pregnant pole vaulters," Three said.

Goldie stared at her for a second. "I got nothing."

"Just commenting on the drunk guys in the corner. They weren't happy to be cut off."

Goldie stared at the Styrofoam boxes. "But, you'll be happy that Wyatt brought you dinner." She pointed to a table. "Go eat. I've got this."

Three sighed. "I don't think I'll ever get this."

"You will, but not before you wear a keg of beer."

Wyatt picked up the to-go containers and moved to a nearby table. "It's Salisbury steak night."

"You bought me dinner?"

"That was the plan, but Riley sent them over on the house."

"Geez, what's up with this town?" she asked.

"Don't complain, just chow down." He opened one box and breathed in the smell of the dark brown gravy.

Though the drunks in the corner paid Goldie and walked outside, Wyatt worried they'd come back. "Are you and Goldie closing the bar?"

"Cannon will come to close up at midnight." She opened the container and grinned. "Oh my God, mashed potatoes too?"

He pointed to the box. "And green beans. Eat your veggies."

"Yes, Dad."

He stabbed a bite with a plastic fork. "Calling me Dad makes that kiss we shared, so wrong."

"You mean that kiss you took."

"Yep, that's the one." He still felt bad, but at least it made for good bantering material.

They ate in silence. It wasn't because they had nothing to say, it was just that the meal was too good not to eat while it was hot.

"Thank you for feeding me again." She collected their empty boxes. "You're far too nice to me."

"Someone has to be."

She said nothing, but her smile said it all. "I have to go back to work."

"I'll leave you be." He paid for his beer and left her a hefty tip. When he walked out, he didn't drive back to the ranch. Instead, he moved his truck to the back of the bar and parked beside Three's SUV. He set his alarm for eleven forty-five and fell asleep.

When his alarm sounded, he stepped out and leaned against the passenger door waiting for her to come out.

Goldie and Three walked out at the top of the hour.

"Looks like you have company," Goldie said.

Three moved toward her SUV. "What are you doing here?"

"Bunkmates creed," he said. "Leave no one behind."

"That's not the bunkmates creed." She opened her door. "You're crazy."

"I've been called worse."

"So have I."

CHAPTER ELEVEN

Her alarm went off before the sun peeked over the horizon. She rolled out of bed and into her boots. The long shirt she'd slept in hung within an inch of her knees. She didn't know who it had belonged to, but they had great taste in music.

Staying in a bunkhouse was like living in a dorm where the musical tastes varied from old rock to country. The person who had this shirt had loved the Eagles, but who didn't?

On a normal day, she would have been up mucking stalls, but nothing had been normal since she'd left Texas. She pulled reins, not taps. She usually smelled like hay and sunshine, but this morning she smelled like an unbathed drunk on a three-day bender. It would depress her if there wasn't a sparkle of light and laughter named Wyatt.

It was because of him she was up at four in the morning, making her way to the kitchen, attempting to pay it forward. She could nap before work, but he would be up and out of the house just as the sun inched over the horizon. The silly man had stayed out way past his bedtime to make sure she got home safely. Who did that?

Why did the strangers in Aspen Cove show more care and consideration than her brother? She trudged into the bathroom to splash water on her face and tie her hair into a ponytail. Her boots shuffled across the worn wooden floors into the kitchen. She figured breakfast was needed and would be appreciated. The only problem was her lack of skill. She considered eggs and bacon, but there weren't any. The muffin would have been a great idea if she hadn't already eaten it. She had half a brownie, but a cowboy couldn't get far if his internal fuel tank was low.

In the cupboard, she found a box of oatmeal. It was a solid breakfast that stuck to the gut for a few hours. Standing before the front of the stove, she mixed the ingredients and followed the directions to a T. The finished product didn't resemble the creamy smooth texture on the box but a thick, clumpy mess.

There weren't any add-ins like brown sugar or nuts. She plopped a glob into a bowl and hoped he would come out soon. She continued to scout for anything to make it taste better. All she found was a tub of margarine.

Inspiration hit her, and she raced back to her bedroom to get the brownie. Without another sweetener, this was the best she could do. She put a dab in the center of the bowl and crumbled the brownie on top. Leaning against the counter, she waited another five minutes.

Worried he'd slept in, she debated delivering breakfast to his door. Noise came from the hallway. Relief washed over her because she wouldn't have to deliver. But what if it was Tom? Did she want him to know she'd cooked Wyatt breakfast?

After a quick thought about actions and consequences, she decided any interaction with Tom was unwelcome and unwise. She swiped the bowl from the counter, picked up a spoon, and hurried to Wyatt's door. A light tap got no response.

When the door handle to the bathroom across the hall turned, she threw caution to the wind and stepped inside Wyatt's room. She didn't know who was coming out of the bathroom, but if it was Tom, she didn't want to be standing at Wyatt's door.

His room was dark. So dark she couldn't see in front of her. "Wyatt?" She moved forward. "Wyatt, are you asleep?"

She inched forward until her knees hit the bed. She breathed deeply and held her breath, hoping to hear something. Not only was the room pitch black, but it was dead silent. The only sign anyone was there was the soft musk that filled the air. She exhaled and then breathed him back in. Most men she knew smelled of sweat and cow shit, but he smelled like Christmas trees and sunshine.

She leaned over to feel the bed, and as she stretched to touch the sheets, the door swung open, and a body was backlit from the hallway light. Startled, she fell onto the mattress. Quick thinking and good balance allowed her to keep the bowl upright.

"Three? Is that you?" He flipped on the light switch.

"Yep." She tugged at the T-shirt riding up her thighs to give a glimpse of her one and only pair of underwear. She struggled to sit up.

"What are you doing here?" He stood before her dressed in a towel wrapped loosely around his hips.

She lifted the bowl and spoon into the air. "I brought you breakfast."

She knew she shouldn't stare, but how was she supposed to ignore the body in front of her? He was sculpted by hours in the saddle. His firm chest, honed by roping, led to solid abs. She silently counted the cans and came up with a six-pack. Her eyes followed the deep V of muscles that disappeared into the terry cloth.

He stepped inside and closed the door.

"You made me breakfast?"

She shrugged. "Don't expect much. I'm not known for my culinary skills." She thrust the bowl forward. In the five minutes since she'd sprinkled the brownie on top, it had sunk into the oatmeal, turning it murky. She lowered her head. "I wanted to say thank you for being considerate."

He sat beside her and took the bowl from her hands. "What is this?"

"Can't you see it's oatmeal?" She wished she could have come up with a creative name, but what would she call something that looked like chunky throw up?

"Yes, I can see it resembles oatmeal, but what are the brown specks?"

She dipped the spoon in and scooped up a bite. "It's the brownie I owed you. Now open up."

He stared at the spoon. "I'm afraid."

She took the first bite. It had the texture of clay. She chewed and swallowed. "It's awful, but it won't kill you."

He grabbed the spoon and took a mouthful.

He moved it around a few times before swallowing. "It is awful, but maybe the best breakfast I've had in a long time."

She narrowed her eyes. "How can it be awful and yet the best thing?"

He forced another bite and smiled. "You made it. You

got up early and cooked me something. That makes it taste a hundred times better."

"A hundred times better than awful is still bad."

He ate another bite. Each time his eyes grew wide, and his throat bobbed with the forced swallow. "It's total shit, Three, but I will finish it because you took the time to make it when you could have slept in. And you delivered it."

She pulled at the T-shirt, so it covered her knees. "There wasn't anything to put on top to sweeten it."

"I see a shopping trip in my future. I'll pick up sugar and milk and raisins."

She made a retching sound. "I hate raisins. They look like animal poop."

"No way, that would be the mini meatballs in canned spaghetti." He scooped up the last bite and set the bowl on the dresser. "Thank you for being thoughtful." He turned toward her, and the towel slipped off his thigh.

His legs were solid and covered in coarse dark hair. The muscles strained against his skin as if begging to be set free from their confines. She took him in from his bare feet to the knot of his towel, which seemed to unravel under her gaze.

"Okay, I just thought I'd do something nice."

He chuckled. "Food poisoning is nice?"

"At least I tried it with a brownie and not arsenic."

He tugged the towel closed. "Thank you. I'm touched."

She rose to her feet and stepped away before his sexiness touched her and she made bad decisions. "I should go. I have a lot to do today."

"Like take a nap?" He adjusted his towel so it wouldn't drop.

96

The action filled her with relief and regret. Her mind said, *Cover that shit up, buddy*, but her body screamed, *Show me more*.

"No, I promised to look in on Cade's horses. When I'm done, I'll nap or drive into Copper Creek and buy underwear." She clapped her hands in excitement. "I made thirty dollars in tips last night."

"I gave you ten."

She smiled. "I know. The rest of the guys were cheap bastards."

"I suppose telling them they were next to be castrated might have something to do with their generosity."

She fisted her hips. "It's a bar, not a brothel. What's wrong with men?"

He stepped toward the door. "They're men."

"But you don't act like that."

"No, but at thirty-six, I'm older and wiser. I've already been verbally castrated a time or two."

She moved to the door. "To be a fly on the wall during those conversations."

He lifted a sexy brow. "So, you're a voyeur."

She stood tall and jutted out her chin. "Never considered it, but ... I'm trying new things. Last week I wouldn't have thought I'd be serving beer in a small-town bar."

"Hunger does crazy things to us, doesn't it?"

There were many hungers in life. Starving for love and affection were two. Respect and consideration were at the top of many people's lists. Passion. Peace. Companionship. Understanding. Those hungers gnawed at a person's insides far longer than an empty stomach.

She opened the door and kissed him on the cheek. "Yes, it does." When she pivoted to walk away, she bumped into Tom.

"Didn't take you long, did it?" he said.

"It's not what you think." She had no place to go. Wyatt was at her back and Tom at her front.

"It's always what I think."

She pushed against Tom's chest. "What you think is shit. Might serve you well to pull your head from your ass."

"Enough, Tom," Wyatt said. "It was just breakfast."

"Is that what she's calling it these days?" He moved down the hallway, leaving them alone.

Wyatt spun her around to face him. "You and I know what happened here."

She nodded. "It's the same everywhere I go."

He pressed a kiss to her forehead. "No good deed ever goes unpunished."

"You're right, but I'm so tired of taking the beatings." She turned and walked away.

"What are you going to do now?"

"I promised to look in on Cade's horses. After that, I'll bury my head in my pillow and sleep. What about you?"

"I'm heading to Lloyd's because if I stay here any longer, I might kick his ass."

She walked back and gave him a hug. "I appreciate your friendship, but I'm not worth fighting over." She spun around and went back to her room. Just before the door clicked shut, she heard his reply.

"You're wrong. I'd fight for you any day."

CHAPTER TWELVE

It had been two days since she made him breakfast. For two more nights, he waited outside the bar to make sure she got home safely.

He dragged himself out of the shower and toweled his wet hair. He couldn't keep this up long-term, or he'd die of exhaustion, but he hated that Three didn't have anyone to be her protector.

She reminded him each night she was thirty years old and well past the need for a babysitter. He disagreed. Criminals didn't put an age limit on their victims.

He always loved an underdog but didn't expect to find the one in Aspen Cove dressed in ill-fitting jeans and T-shirts.

When he walked out of the bathroom with a towel wrapped around his waist, she was standing there with two cups of coffee. How she looked so spry and beautiful, he couldn't fathom. She'd had the same amount of sleep he had, but he felt like the dung found on the soles of his boots.

"You're up early."

"I'm off today." She thrust a cup into his hands.

He threw her a sideways look but took the mug and drank deeply. She might not be able to make good oatmeal, but she made excellent coffee.

"I thought you'd be sleeping in."

Tom shuffled out of his room and pushed his way past her. She held up her cup so it wouldn't spill.

"Take it in the bedroom and leave the hallway free of your bullshit, Trinity." He slammed the bathroom door behind him.

"He's a real asshole. What did you do to him again?" Wyatt asked.

She smiled. "I wouldn't do him." She turned around and walked toward the kitchen. "Breakfast is on the table. I'll be outside feeding the horses."

All he could think about was her first try at cooking for him. He ate every bite because she'd made the effort, but his stomach couldn't take another round of Three's creative cooking.

To his surprise, what he found was a plate of apple spice muffins. He refilled his mug and swiped all three because Tom didn't deserve any of her sweetness.

He left the cabin and climbed inside his truck, setting the muffins and the mug of coffee on the dash. At the turn of his key, the passenger door opened, and Three climbed inside.

"What are you doing?"

She laughed. "If you can follow me at my job, I'm returning the favor."

"You afraid someone will be inappropriate? Are you trying to defend my honor?"

She turned to face him while he pulled away from the

bunkhouse. "I got your back. I hear you're having an issue with a young flower."

"Violet is a pain in my ass. If you were like that as a young girl, I can see why everyone says you're trouble." He tossed her a muffin and grabbed one for himself. "Thanks for breakfast."

"You're welcome." She peeled off the paper cup and traded him muffins. "If you think my oatmeal tasted awful, try eating the paper baking cup."

He took a bite, and at the turn on to the main road he stopped and looked at her. "Were you?"

She grabbed his mug of coffee to wash down her last bite. "Was I what?"

"Like Violet?"

"I imagine in some ways I was." She handed him his coffee. "I was a young impressionable girl. I had a crush or two on a handsome cowboy."

"You think I'm handsome?"

"I wasn't talking about you, but yes, I think you'll do in a pinch." She picked the raisins from her muffin and tossed them out the window.

"That's littering."

"I'm composting. It's only littering if the earth doesn't eat it in a timely manner. Give it one rain and a hot day, and those nasty things will disappear."

"Do you like grapes?"

He could see her roll her eyes out of the side of his. "I've heard the argument before. I like grapes, but not a fan of them dried out. They remind me of guinea pig poop."

"But they taste better."

"How would you know?"

"I don't, but I'd say it's a safe bet. Now back to you

and those cowboys. Tell me about living your life in a bunkhouse."

"When I was born, my father was a ranch hand on the Mercer Ranch near Lone Tree. My mom took off when I was little. Their cook did a lot of babysitting. The day I could attend school must have been the happiest day of my father's life. His second happiest was probably when I left McKinley Ranch."

"I doubt that. Now tell me how a girl survives the bunkhouse." He wanted to hear her story. It couldn't have been easy. He thought about his sister and what it would have been like for him to live with her in a house full of men. Anyone with a lick of sense would have pretended she didn't exist if they didn't want to die.

She settled back and sighed. "Early on, it was easy. We had a cabin at the Mercer's. It was in a group of cabins where the ranch hands stayed. Awesome digs, actually. You rarely live in a single-family home while working a ranch for someone else. When Mr. Mercer died, we found ourselves in a different situation because of the foreman."

"You left Colorado for Wyoming." He turned on the country road leading to Lloyd's.

"They had bunkhouses. I always had the top bunk above my father, and my brothers' bunk was beside ours. No one was getting near me. By then, I was a teenager, but I had all the parts of a woman."

"Trouble."

She nodded. "Yep, because I didn't know what that did to men. My poor brothers had bloody knuckles for the first month on the ranch. It was okay for several years. There were guys that pushed their luck, but after a few of the cowboys sported black eyes, no one bothered me until

Luke left. By then, I was in my twenties. That was when trouble started."

He parked the truck and turned to her. "You weren't the trouble?"

"No, I was a girl who attracted men without trying. I had the right parts. You stick twenty men in a room and put one girl in there, she could look like a toad covered with warts, and there would be problems. The rest is history. I never asked for their attention. I didn't go out of my way to attract it. I never had a bad reputation until those three showed up. Two of them were harmless, but Tom, he was the instigator."

"He's definitely not a fan of yours. Shall we go?" He grabbed his backpack. He'd filled it with canned meat and a package of burger buns the day before. He rounded the truck and met her on the passenger side. "Ready to be a cattle rancher?"

"What are we doing today?"

"Inventory. The books need to be straight."

"We're counting cattle?"

"Sort of. We're tagging cattle. Lloyd invested in an RFID system."

"And my job?"

"Since I didn't know you were coming, we'll figure it out as we go." He wrapped his arm around her shoulder and led her into the barn.

"Will Lloyd care if I'm here?"

He chuckled. "I've never heard of someone complaining about free labor. Saddle up Red."

She moved like a lightning bolt to his horse. Red turned around and nuzzled her neck. "He's a sweet boy."

"You are trouble. That horse doesn't like anyone but me and now you."

"Is that a problem?"

"Not for me."

"Someone got a problem in here?" A deep voice came from the door. If he didn't know what Lloyd looked like, he would have put Sam Elliot's face to this drawl.

"No, sir." He moved toward Lloyd. "I hope you don't mind, but Trinity Mosier is tagging along."

Violet walked inside the stable and rolled her eyes. "Does it matter if I mind?"

Her father pointed to the stall with her horse. "Basil left an hour ago to set up the chute."

"Baz, Dad. He likes the name Baz."

Lloyd narrowed his eyes. "I like Elvis or Brad Pitt, but that ain't my name." He tossed a bag of supplies to Wyatt then looked at Three. "Can you ride?"

"Yes, sir. I'm a horse trainer by trade."

Lloyd nodded. "Is that so?" He looked toward a stall at the end. "I might have a job for you. Whiskey has a biting habit. Think you might like to work with him?"

Wyatt watched her eyes light up. "I'd love to." She pulled the collar of her T-shirt over her shoulder to show a large scar. "I've got some experience with a biter."

Lloyd walked over to see the extent of her injury. "That's some bite. What happened to the horse?"

"After training, he never bit me again. I had him until two years ago when I had to put him down."

Lloyd nodded. "I'll pay you fifteen an hour."

She smiled so wide Wyatt was certain she'd split her cheeks. "I would have done it for free."

"Free doesn't buy you food or clothes," Lloyd said. "Today, you'll get ten an hour since it doesn't take nothing special to tag a cow."

She shook her head. "Today, I'll work for free since you weren't expecting me."

Lloyd grunted and grabbed his saddle. In minutes, they were moving toward pasture six. It was closest to the house and easiest for Baz to set up the chute.

Violet rode beside her father, but she threw murderous looks toward Three the whole way.

When they arrived, they began the long task of tagging over three hundred head of cattle. Baz and Lloyd led them into the chute. Three calmed them with her sweet voice and gentle touch while Violet swabbed their ears. He tagged them and let them loose.

It was well after lunch when they broke for a meal. The Lloyds headed back to their house. He and Three were invited to join them, but he wasn't in the mood to share her with anyone and declined.

"You hungry?" He climbed on top of Rex. "I know a great place to eat."

She mounted Red, and he led her to the copse of trees on the far end of the field. They found a patch of grass to relax on while he made them deviled ham sandwiches. Canned meat wasn't anything special, but it was protein and traveled easily in his saddlebag.

"Oh, Wyatt, you sure know how to treat a girl," she teased when he handed her a flattened bun filled with pink mush.

He made to swipe it back, but she rolled out of his way. "No way, this is my favorite. Spam comes in second place, but I like it grilled until the outside is crispy."

He held up a finger. "I also have dessert." He reached into the bag and withdrew a package of peanut butter cups.

"Oh. My. God. I'd do just about anything for one of those."

He lifted a brow. "Anything?"

"Just about." She bit into her sandwich and moaned. He'd do anything to hear that sound again.

They chatted about horses and ranch life while they ate. He didn't want to like Three as much as he did. Not that she was trouble; all women were in his book. Hell, she'd already stolen hours of sleep from him. Now she was working on stealing something else—his good sense. He desperately wanted to lean over and give her a real kiss, but they had to get back to the cows.

They worked until the sun glowed orange behind Mt. Meeker. When they returned to the stables, they took care of the horses.

"You did a great job," he said.

She smiled. "I love this life. I'd rather spend an entire day in the saddle than anywhere else. Serving beers at the Brewhouse is going to kill me."

"Me too." He moved toward her so he stood close enough to feel the heat coming from her body. "You are trouble, Three. Big trouble for me." He touched her shoulders and brushed his lips against hers.

She glanced around. "Is Violet coming?"

"I don't know, and I don't care." He stared at her plump pink lips. Her tongue darted out to wet them. Even at thirty, he was certain she didn't fully understand her allure. She didn't have sex appeal. She was sex appeal packaged in a cowgirl's body.

When her hand came up to rest against his chest, adrenaline coursed through him. He wanted this kiss like he wanted his next breath or beer or meal. She closed the distance between them and tilted her head upward. All he needed was to bend down and cover that sexy mouth with his. When he did, he was unprepared for the heat that burned inside him. When she let him in, everything turned molten. A quiet moan escaped her lips, telling him she liked the kiss as much as he did. Backing up, she hit the wall, but he didn't let up his thorough exploration of her mouth.

He growled as he deepened the kiss and tasted her in long, lush licks. She met him with equal vigor. With her hands roping around his waist, she moved until they were body to body. Awareness of her curves pressing against him created a need to touch every inch. His hands moved from her shoulders to her waist. Just as he was about to grip her back end, someone cleared their throat, and he stepped away from Three.

"Get a room," Violet said. She marched her horse to the end of the stable.

"Ready to go home?" he asked Three.

"Are you cooking dinner?"

"I've got chili dogs and chips." He slid his hand across her back and walked her to the truck.

Before she got inside, she looked at him and asked, "Are you sure that kiss wasn't because of Violet?"

His palms pressed flat to the door on either side of her head, caging her in.

"The first time I kissed you, I was faking it for Violet." He leaned until her breath tickled his chin. "This time was for real—for me."

CHAPTER THIRTEEN

She opened her drawer to see a dozen pairs of underwear. It was the little things that made the biggest difference: a smile, a wave hello, a trip to Target, a day without seeing Tom. Those were the tiny nuggets of joy that made a hard life livable. There were also long walks with Wyatt. Stolen kisses in the stables and longing looks when he walked her to her bedroom each night before he turned to go to his.

It had been almost two weeks since that first real kiss. Fourteen days filled with hard work, that were rewarded with kisses. Lots of kisses.

She'd spent several of those days working with Whiskey. She figured his problem came from boredom more than anything else. He nipped at her a few times, but a quick lesson in respect had him behaving. A few minutes a day establishing personal space and defining the rules was all he needed. Too bad men weren't as easy to train. She pictured taking a lunge whip to Tom each time he crossed the line. The vision made her laugh.

She moved Whiskey back and forward, always keeping him questioning her next move.

"You are a horse whisperer," Violet said.

It was odd to hear her speak anything but complaints. "He's a good boy. I think he's bored. You should ride him."

She shrugged. "He was my mom's and hasn't been ridden in years. She stopped riding several years before she passed away."

"I heard your mother was an excellent horsewoman."

Violet leaned against the split-rail fence. "Who told you?"

She tied Whiskey to the rail and joined Violet by the fence.

"Your sister, Poppy. She comes into the Brewhouse with Mark sometimes. I like her."

Violet lifted her shoulders. "She's all right, I guess."

"What about you? What do you do in your spare time?"

Like every other petulant teen, she rolled her eyes. "What spare time? I'm a rancher's daughter. Even if I had free time, I'm under the watchful eye of my father and brother. I mean, how's a girl supposed to get good at kissing if she can't meet any boys?"

Trinity laughed. "That is a problem."

"You have no idea."

"You'd be surprised." She checked the time. It was almost lunchtime, and she needed to meet Wyatt on the range, but she understood Violet and thought she could offer some words of wisdom. "You want to spend your lunch hour in town at the diner? My treat."

"Seriously? You're inviting me to lunch?"

"Sure, why not?"

Violet kicked the dirt under her feet. "I haven't been nice to you."

"We all have bad days. Ask your dad if you can go."

She sent him a text and got the go-ahead. "It's a date."

"Can you follow me into town? I have to work tonight. After we eat, I need to go home and change. It will save me time if I don't need to come back here beforehand."

"Sure, I'll meet you at Maisey's." She cocked her head to the side. "What about Wyatt?"

"What about him?"

She frowned. "You guys disappear each day at lunch to do God knows what."

Trinity laughed. "We disappear to eat."

"Right. Code for—"

"No code, usually peanut butter and jelly or canned ham spread."

She took the reins and led Whiskey into the stables. Violet followed her.

"Gross."

"See, you're doing me a favor and saving me from another sandwich." That wasn't the case, but something told Trinity that Violet needed her time more than Wyatt.

Once Whiskey got settled, they climbed into their cars and took off toward Maisey's. Trinity called Wyatt on the way. He was disappointed, but the one thing she'd learned over the years was that men were a lot like horses. They were stubborn and often aggressive, and they'd push you to see how far they could go. But, in her experience, defining boundaries and setting the tone was important. It wasn't wise to let a man manipulate anything, including her time.

They entered Maisey's and took a booth by the window.

After ordering blue plate specials, Trinity said, "You know, Violet, I'm not all that different from you."

Violet made a sound like she was clearing her throat. "You've got Wyatt."

She couldn't argue there. She had Wyatt or at least his kisses. "He was too old for you. He's almost too old for me."

Violet's eyes widened. "How old are you?"

"Thirty, and Wyatt's thirty-six. You should set your eyes on boys closer to your age. They'll be more fun in the long run. Wouldn't you like to be with a young man who likes what you do?"

"I suppose." She pursed her lips. "Besides doing the dirty, what do you and Wyatt do?"

Trinity wanted to laugh, but she'd been eighteen once, and very little was humorous at that age.

"Contrary to what you think, Wyatt and I aren't doing the dirty, as you call it. I have too much respect for myself to jump between the sheets with just any man."

"He's not any man. He's Wyatt Morrison. Are we talking about the same guy here?" She leaned in. "Over six feet tall, broad shoulders, eyelashes wasted on a man, and lips that look pillow soft?"

The laugh bubbled up despite her attempts to swallow it down. "Same man. Still too old for you."

She sighed. "You're right. I know it, but it's okay to dream, right? I mean it's like watching a movie star. You know you'll never date him, but sometimes the fantasy is almost as good as the reality."

Trinity had never been a big sister, but there were

times she wished she'd had one. Poor Violet had four of them, but they were mostly absent.

"Honey, the fantasy is always better than the reality."

"You have no idea what it's like living on a ranch with a dad and a brother."

Maisey brought their meals. "You two need anything else?"

"We're good," Trinity said. "Maybe pie after?" When Maisey walked away, she turned her attention back to Violet. "You're wrong. I know exactly what you're going through. I grew up on ranches. Only I had a father and two brothers but no mother. I see that shotgun sitting by the front door at your house. Imagine having three of them at the ready each time you left to go anywhere."

Her eyes grew saucer wide. "How did you survive?"

She wondered if she had. "Your dad and your brother are trying to protect you. There are a lot of creepy men out there." She thought about Tom. "Many men would take what you're not offering. Several would accept what you are even when they know they shouldn't. Do you understand what I'm saying?"

"Yes. Men are idiots."

"Some, but not all." Trinity took a bite of her meat-loaf. "It's important to stand back and look deeper than a man's height, his broad shoulders, and his lips."

"You're talking about Wyatt."

"Yes, but I'm only pointing out what attracted you to him."

Violet frowned. "How long did you know him before you kissed him?"

There was no way Trinity would answer that question. "My relationship with Wyatt is irrelevant. We were talking about our fathers and brothers and how hard they can make dating or relationships."

"I'll die a spinster."

Trinity almost spit out her bite of mashed potatoes. "No, you won't. Let me tell you what not to do. Don't sneak around. I did that, and it got me a bad reputation. One I didn't deserve."

"Were you at a big ranch with lots of hotties?"

"Yes, but I never dated anyone at the ranch where I lived. Don't mix mattresses with money. I'd also add that you shouldn't date people who work for competitors. That was my mistake."

She nodded. "Any more words of wisdom?"

"I've got plenty. With men, go slow. They'll respect you more, and it will give you time to decide if they're worthy of you. Never let a man make you feel like you're less. People lie, but you know the truth. It's more important to respect yourself. I don't know much about love. I've never been in love, but I have a feeling you don't have to look for it, it often finds you. At least that's how it worked for my brothers."

"You're a lot nicer than I thought." Violet moved her gravy around her plate. "I'm sorry I was bitchy to you."

"Don't worry about it. I get why you didn't like me."

"My mom would reach down from heaven and smack me upside the head if she could. She always said to not judge a book by its cover. It was important to look inside the pages to see what was really there."

Trinity pushed her plate aside. "Your mom sounds like she was a wonderful woman. Her lessons will always be there, whispering in your ear."

"I hear her all the time."

"You're lucky. Listen to her counsel, and when you

can't hear her, listen to your gut. Believe what your heart tells you, not what others say."

"Good advice." She paused for a second. "What happened to your mom?"

The mention of her mother always made her sad. "I don't really know, but according to my dad, she left because she didn't like our way of life."

"Do you miss her?"

"Can't miss what you never had."

Maisey walked to the booth. "How about that pie?"

Violet shook her head and patted her stomach. "Full as a tick. Can't eat another bite."

They both looked at Trinity. "I'm tapping out too." She paid their bill, and they walked outside. "I've got to go to work, but I'll see you tomorrow. I'll show you how to tame a beast."

TRINITY WALKED INSIDE to find Sage behind the register. She'd only met her a few times but liked her.

"Are you working with me tonight?" Trinity asked.

"Not a chance. I'm only holding down the fort until Cannon gets back with pizza. We have an announcement. It will probably be a busy night because the first round is on us."

"Wow, that must be quite an announcement." Trinity moved behind the bar and started filling bowls with bar mix. "Is Goldie coming in tonight too?"

"To drink, maybe, but not to work. You're on your own."

Trinity swallowed her disappointment. She sucked at cocktail waitressing. With a ten percent spill average, she was surprised she still had a job. The people of Aspen Cove were far too kind, but she imagined they had their limits. Luckily, she hadn't reached the threshold to get canned yet.

"I'd start pulling pitchers right away and set them on the counter if I were you. That way, you're ahead of the game." Sage turned green and ran to the back before Trinity could ask about the announcement.

She pulled pitchers as suggested until a rowdy bunch of construction workers came inside. It wasn't the Coopers or the Lockharts. She'd met both groups of brothers and found them to be polite and charming. This was a crew subcontracted to one of Wes Covington's companies, and they were an inch away from getting gelded each time they came into the place.

"What will it be, guys?" She asked from a safe distance because if she got too close, they massaged her ass like a side of Kobe beef. She'd only put up with so much groping before noses bled, and eyes got blackened. The one good thing about growing up on a ranch full of men was learning how to fight dirty.

"Two pitchers and you."

She rolled her eyes. "Does that work at the other bars around?"

"Works at Buttercups." He pulled a stack of ones from his pocket. "If I shoved these down your pants, would I get a happy ending?"

She shook her head. "You'd get an ending, but it would come with a tombstone and a eulogy." She picked up the beer and glasses and set them on the table.

The door opened and in walked Cannon, followed by a crowd. She hurried to the bar and filled up more pitchers. Within fifteen minutes, she was certain anyone within drinking age was around to hear whatever Cannon had to say. Doc and Agatha walked inside with a man who looked far too sophisticated to be a resident of Aspen Cove. They sat at the bar. Last to walk in was Wyatt. Each time she saw him, her heart had a conference with her head, telling her brain it was okay to love.

He leaned over the bar and gave her a quick peck on the lips before he took a seat next to the stranger.

Cannon jumped on a barstool and called Sage over. They were married, so a wedding wasn't in the cards. With the way Sage clutched onto the empty white bucket and a package of Saltines, it could only be one thing.

"Just a quick announcement." Cannon looked down at his wife. "I wanted everyone to know that Sage and I are having a baby." He smiled like a goofball. "She's having the baby, but I put it there." He pounded on his chest and smiled. "First round is on us."

The crowd erupted into hoots and hollers.

"You want some help?" Wyatt asked. "You pour them, and I'll deliver."

She knew she liked him. Not only was he a good kisser, but he wasn't afraid of working.

She filled up several pitchers, and he put them on tables. She turned to Doc, Agatha, and the stranger.

"What can I get you? Beer is free." She slid a pitcher and three glasses before they could answer.

Agatha smiled. "I'm a wine drinker. Do you think you can sneak me a glass?"

"No sneaking allowed, but I'll get you a glass. Cannon said first round is on him. Even if it wasn't, I'd put this one on my tab." She leaned in toward the older woman. "Did you know you were the first person in town who was kind to me?"

"I'm sure it was because you stopped into the pharmacy before going anywhere else." Agatha turned to the man beside her. "This is Jake Powers. He'll be hanging out in town for a while."

"Just a while?"

The man eyed the ruckus behind him. "Yes, I have some business to attend to, and then I'll be on my way."

Trinity held out her hand. "Nice to meet you, Jake Powers. I hope you change your mind. There's something special about Aspen Cove."

In the corner, the rowdies held up a pitcher. She poured another, and Wyatt delivered. She could hear one man tell him to send her over because they wanted to renegotiate their lap dance.

He laughed it off, but she knew he wasn't happy. It showed in his stiff shoulders and cold stare.

"Can I kick them out?" he asked as he took his stool at the bar.

"Nope. Not your bar. Cannon's here, so he'll deal with them if they get out of hand."

Katie arrived with a box of muffins and a plate of brownies. The muffins were for Trinity. The brownies were for Sage, who had serious chocolate cravings.

Katie sidled up to Trinity. "Who's the new guy?" She nodded toward Jake.

"His name is Jake Powers, but I don't know why he's in town. Seems to be cozy with Doc and Agatha."

"Oh my God, he's probably the new owner of the dry goods store. Find out what you can." Katie spun around and joined her husband, Bowie, who sat with Dalton and Samantha. Trinity wondered if Cannon's father was a mercenary or an assassin given the names of his children.

Maybe baking at Katie's and cooking at Maisey's was his cover.

Trinity wasn't a fan of beating around the bush so she approached him and said, "You must be the new owner of the dry goods store. Care to say what you're putting in?"

Jake looked at Agatha and Doc. They both shook their heads.

"Nope, it's a secret." He put a ten on the counter and slid from his seat. "I've got to get going. Nice to meet you, Trinity." He held her hand a moment too long.

She watched Wyatt's eyes turn feral, and his expression possessive.

"You too."

By ten o'clock, the bar was nearly empty except the rowdies who'd eaten enough pizza to sober them up for round two.

Trinity leaned over the bar to talk to Wyatt, who was fading. "You should go home. You can't babysit me all the time."

"I'm not leaving you here alone with them."

She glanced around. She wasn't alone. She had Mike the one-eyed cat and a couple of Dalton's biker friends. They looked like murderers, but they were harmless.

"I can take care of myself."

Wyatt shook his head.

A guy from the trouble table raised several twenties into the air.

"Looks like they're on their way out."

He spun around to watch as she walked to the group.

"Are you ready to go?" she asked when she approached.

He grabbed her by the waist and pulled her into his lap. She fisted up to hit when Wyatt yanked her free. It all happened so fast. The first fist split the air, and before she knew it, a bar brawl broke out. By the time Sheriff Cooper arrived, the rowdies were crumbled in a heap on the floor, two chairs were broken, and Cannon was staring at her with a look she knew all too well. It was the same look Mr. McKinley had given her the day he asked her to leave the ranch.

She threw up her hands. "I know. I'm fired."

Cannon frowned. "Trinity, I'm not firing you."

"Okay, well then, I quit."

She picked up her purse and walked out the back to her SUV.

"Three, wait up."

She spun around and held up her hand. "No. You don't get to say you're sorry."

He shook his head. "I'm not. Those guys had it coming. He touched what was mine."

Her mouth dropped open. "What are you, a dog, and I'm your bone?"

"You know what I mean."

"Yeah, I do. You're as big an idiot as they were. I told you I could take care of myself. If you would have given me ten more seconds, it would have been fine."

"He was pawing you."

She could feel the heat rising to her cheeks. "He was an asshole, and I was handling it."

He marched forward until he stood toe to toe with her. "No, he was handling you, and I don't share."

"Newsflash, Wyatt. I don't belong to anyone. I belong to me." She pounded her fist against her chest. "You just cost me my job and the respect of everyone in this town. Rumor had it, I was trouble. You've just proven I am."

She climbed into her SUV and took off toward home.

CHAPTER FOURTEEN

One miserable week had passed. Each day he waited in his truck, hoping she'd hop inside and tell him he was forgiven, but all he'd received was the silent treatment.

This morning he found her at Cade's stable. He'd recently expanded it with the help of the Coopers. They donated the kit and the labor because it was the first earth-friendly stable they'd erected.

"Trinity. Please talk to me."

She ignored him and continued to hang the tack in the supply room.

"We live together. Eventually, you'll have to say something."

She huffed and turned around. "I don't have much to say, Wyatt, but I have a lot of work to do." She brushed past him and took Sable from the stable to saddle her.

"You riding your brother's horse today? You know, Red misses you."

She placed the saddle blanket, hoisted the saddle to Sable's back and cinched it tight. "Give him a carrot for me. I don't have any reason to be on the Dawsons' ranch."

"Violet is asking about you. You've made an impression on her. What do I tell her?"

She stuck her foot in the stirrup. "Tell her to call me." She lifted herself into the saddle.

"She asked me if I had been an idiot."

"Did you tell her, yes?"

"I did, and she told me to speak to your heart."

She nudged the horse forward. "That will be impossible. It's not that I'm heartless, but I'm listening to my heart less."

He chased after her and found her walking the horse toward Tom. "You're working with him?"

She stopped and turned around. "I don't have much choice if I want a roof over my head and a meal in my stomach. The one thing I hate the most is not having choices." She shook her head. "Actually, it's having them limited by others."

She took off toward Tom, and his heart sank. Because of him, she was forced to spend her days in the saddle beside a man worse than the ones at the bar. He'd turned her life from awful to horrific.

———

THE NEXT MORNING, he waited in the kitchen with bacon and eggs. She thanked him and left. The following day he made her pancakes.

"Why are you doing this?" she asked.

"Because I screwed up."

Tom rushed by and grabbed a pancake from her plate. "Thanks for breakfast, asshole." He shoved it in his mouth and rushed out the door.

"Are you still working with him?"

"Still need a roof over my head."

"I'll take care of you." He hated the way Tom had turned smug over the last few days. How he tortured him with talk about how he spent the day riding with Trinity, and how nice her ass looked in the saddle.

Each time Tom goaded him, he fisted up but kept his hands tight to his sides. Any fight on the Mosier Ranch would get him booted, and Trinity didn't take kindly to him interfering.

"I promised my brother I'd help. Thank you for teaching me how to move cattle. At least I bring some value to this ranch."

He moved closer. All he wanted was to pull her into his arms. To press his lips against her and melt into a kiss. "You're not useless. You're everything, Trinity. Don't let any man make you feel less. You're so much more."

"I know." She put her half-eaten plate in the sink. "I've got to go, or Tom will complain. Thanks for breakfast."

"Trinity, you know I'd give you anything."

Her lips stretched into a tight line. "Why? What do you want from me?"

"Everything." He moved to her side and cupped her cheek. "I don't get many good things in my life, and you're the one good thing that I want." He risked a kiss and stepped away. "Be safe out there. It's supposed to storm this afternoon."

She walked to the door. Instead of stepping out, she looked over her shoulder. "You be safe too. I'll see you later."

As soon as she closed the door, he thanked the heavens. At least she was talking to him. That first week of silence was pure torture. She'd opened the door a tiny bit, and he wanted to squeeze himself inside.

When he got to Lloyd's, he was feeling confident and happy until he saw an older man in the stable.

"Can I help you?" He walked over. The gray hair and leathered skin of the guy said he'd spent years in the saddle.

"I'm Jimmy. You must be Wyatt."

"I am. Is there something you need?"

"I guess a tour, and a place to put my tack."

Wyatt's mind whirled. Was he being replaced? He knew his head had been elsewhere these past few weeks, but he'd finished his work. He didn't believe in giving anything less than a hundred percent.

"Are you joining the team?"

He nodded. "Yep, I needed a job, and Lloyd told me to come on over. We go back a long way. I've been at the Sutter ranch for years, but they're closing down."

That blew Wyatt's mind. The Sutters had been in the cattle business since Moses parted the Red Sea.

"That's crazy."

"Sign of the times. You don't raise cattle if you want to get rich."

"But nothing satisfies like a bone-in ribeye." He pointed to the door at the end of the stable. "Find a place anywhere inside." He turned to find the paint mare in the end stall. "I see you found an empty stall for your horse." If the man brought his horse and tack, he was staying, which didn't bode well long-term for Wyatt. He already knew he'd never be the foreman of the Big D Ranch, but he didn't expect to keep tumbling down the food chain. "I was going to check the fence. You want to ride along?" Unlike Cade, Lloyd didn't have his property surrounded by galvanized steel. He was working on one pasture at a time.

They saddled their horses in silence. Wyatt threw the man two bottles of cold water before they headed downrange.

"You live at Lloyd's too?" Jimmy asked.

"Nope, I'm housed elsewhere because of his daughters. You?"

"I'm staying in the house for now. I don't see his daughters throwing me much attention. I'm older than their pops."

"Old don't mean you're dead. Word of caution; that shotgun on the porch is loaded."

Jimmy laughed. "Son, I'm sixty-five. I might not be dead, but the body don't work like it used to, and when it functions, it's usually in the most inopportune places. I'd say I'm safe. What about you? You got a filly?"

"I'm not sure." They moved along the fence, looking for breaks. "I thought I did, but then I pissed her off when I started a fight."

"Went all caveman, huh?" He held up a hand that showed a crooked finger. "Busted that one on some guy's jaw when he looked at my date with lust in his eyes."

"What did she do?"

"She took me home and had her way with me, but women are different these days. They say they like strong men, men who take charge. But go all *Fifty Shades* on her, and you'll wake up tied down, doused in kerosene, and her standing there with a match. Women want guitar playing, laundry washing, housecleaning men. Hell, nowadays it's sometimes hard to tell the difference between men and women. What the hell is hair product for men? When did we start using anything but a bar of soap for skincare? We didn't care if our food was poached, broiled, or baked as long as it was plentiful and hot. Now I'm supposed to recite poetry, chop wood and kill a bear with my hands. No, thank you. I'll stick to my horse."

Wyatt laughed. "Killing bears is Cade Mosier's job. The rest I can't answer for. You're right, women are difficult, but find the right one, and she's worth the trouble." He thought of Three, whose birth name was synonymous with triple trouble. If he had to dance in the front yard with a boombox on his shoulder, shave his legs and wear a kilt, or get down on his knees and beg, he would.

They finished early, and Lloyd told Wyatt to go home. It wasn't often they got a day off, so beating Three back to the bunkhouse was a treat. He stopped by the corner store and picked up stuff for dinner and a package of peanut butter cups, which was her favorite. He also got a bouquet.

He wouldn't normally enter anyone's room without permission, but with Tom around, flaunting anything romantic was like poking a wasp's nest. Putting flowers and candy on the table was an invitation to fight. Hell, cooking for her and not Tom was the same, but it wasn't an in the face taunting since he'd set the tone from day one.

It didn't sit right that she had to spend her days with a guy she loathed. Each day he returned home, he found her looking like she wanted to gag and hogtie him. That was when she came out of her room.

He opened the door and breathed in her space. She always smelled like a sunny day if that was a scent. That and flowers or floral shampoo. She didn't leave her stuff in the shower because Tom helped himself to everything. The man had no boundaries.

He set the flowers and candy on her pillow. When he turned, he saw two framed photos. One was of her and her brothers and father. Another was older. Trinity was a child sitting on the hip of a woman who was her doppel-ganger. How awful for her to feel like she wasn't enough for her mother to stay. She had a list of people who let her down, and he refused to be one more.

He closed the door and walked into the bathroom to shower off the range dust. Knowing she would do the same, he wrote on the steamy mirror, *Please go out with me.*

He was in the kitchen when they returned. The chicken was in the oven, and the red potatoes were boil-ing. "I'm making dinner," he said.

"Smells good," Three commented and went into her room.

He smiled because he knew she was looking at the candy and flowers right then.

The next thing he heard was the bathroom door slam and Trinity call Tom a pig. She walked into the kitchen, holding her towel and carrying her shampoo.

"Don't tell me he beat you to the shower?"

"Okay, I won't tell you, but he did."

"Dammit. There was something in there for your eyes only."

"Something else?" She plopped down into a chair at the table. "Thanks for the flowers and candy, but you shouldn't."

He opened the refrigerator and took out two beers. When he twisted the cap off one, he handed it to her. "I should apologize in advance."

"What now?"

He twisted his lips. "You always shower first. I wrote

something on the mirror that would show up when it got steamy, and now he will get it."

She took a long draw of her beer and shrugged. "Unless you're asking him for sexual favors, you should be all right."

He hoped Tom missed the message. The man was oblivious to most things, so the chance was good he wouldn't notice.

When the door opened, Tom traipsed down the hall wearing a towel. He looked at Wyatt and then at Three. "If the message is from you, then the answer is yes, but I pick the place, and it's my mattress." He turned back to him. "If it's from you ... sorry, man, but you're not my type. I've got a date with several pairs of D cups."

"Buttercups?"

"Yep, you want to come?"

Wyatt continued to cut the ends off the green beans he was preparing. "No thanks, man. Not my style."

Tom swiped a beer from the refrigerator and walked back to his room.

"What did you write on the mirror?" She rose and hurried to the bathroom. When she came back with her hands fisted on her hips, he knew she wasn't happy. "Why would you do that? You know who he is and what he's about. I'm not allowed to date anyone who works on my brother's ranch. If I do, I'll have to leave." She closed her eyes and tightened her features. "I don't have anywhere to go."

He moved to her and set his hands on her shoulders. "I don't work for your brother, and I'd never jeopardize your family situation."

Breath rushed from her lungs. "You're like me. You don't intend to cause trouble, but you do. What is it that you want from me? What do I have to do to get you to stop?"

He pressed his forehead to hers. "Go out with me. Let me show you the kind of man I can be. I'm begging you, please."

One step back, and she looked into his eyes. Was she searching for something? Could she see how much he needed a yes?

"Are you asking me out on a real date? Is that why you bought the flowers and candy?"

He moved closer. "Yes. I've missed you. I really want to do right by you. Kind of feel like it's my job to make up for all the idiots in the world."

"I've dealt with a lot of idiots." Her fingers walked up the buttons of his shirt. When she got to the top, she slid her palms over to rest on his shoulders.

"I was one of them. Give me another chance. We're not breaking any rules. There won't be any more trouble."

"If I say yes, when will this date be?"

"How about Saturday? You dress pretty, and I'll take care of the rest."

She stepped back and turned to walk away.

"Is that a yes?" he called from the kitchen.

She nodded. "It's a yes."

He'd never been so happy in his life. "Dinner will be ready in thirty minutes."

By the time she returned, Tom was gone, and they had the place to themselves. He pulled out all the stops to woo her. He lit a candle Abby had brought over in case of a power outage, which might be a possibility given the storm raging outside.

"Is this normal for this time of year?" she asked.

"The deluge of rain? Yes, it's afternoon storms from

here on out to fall. The worst ones bring hail the size of baseballs, but that usually happens in the foothills. Although I've seen some as big as golf balls here."

"What happens when that hits and you're on the range?"

"You run for cover. Your brother has a storm shelter. I'd suggest you run for it. Let the horses loose. They'll find safety in the trees. If you can't make it home or to the shelter, find someplace to hide until the storm passes."

When they finished their dinner, he insisted on cleaning up while she curled into the chair in the corner with a book. It was a relief to see she didn't hide in her room. He wondered if her nightly absence was because of Tom's presence or her anger at him.

They sat in separate chairs. She read while he watched the storm, and when night fell, he rose. "I'm heading to bed. I've got a long day tomorrow."

"Why is it any longer than the rest?" She set her book on the table and stood.

"Because tomorrow is Friday and the day before our date. It will be the longest day in history."

She graced him with a smile. One that had his heart galloping.

"You'll survive."

He walked her to her bedroom door. "Can I kiss you good night?"

She shook her head. He glimpsed the mischief lighting her eyes. "Not before our first date. Who do you think I am? Trixie from Buttercups?"

He laughed. "I know you're not because if you were, my wallet would be empty. I'd pay anything to see you dance for me."

She cupped his cheek. "I won't dance for you, but I'll dance *with* you."

"It's a date," he said.

"Let's get through our first date before we plan our second." The door swung open, and she stepped inside.

"What if our first date never ends?" he asked.

"Everything ends." She closed the door.

CHAPTER FIFTEEN

Dress pretty, he said. She didn't own pretty or do pretty. Pretty was a flower or a rainbow. She was a cowgirl, and her nice jeans and boots were her dress-up clothes. Nice jeans meant the ones with the smallest holes.

Part of her felt giddy with excitement, part of her filled with dread. She hadn't done much dating in her life. There was Alec Baldwin in high school. Not the movie star but the boy whose father owned the feed store. He used to volunteer for the deliveries to McKinley Ranch. That was fourteen years ago. Since then, most of her encounters had been with cowboys on the circuit. After the rodeo, they'd all meet in the local bar and celebrate or commiserate. She'd helped one or two of the nicer guys feel slightly better for their loss.

The people of Aspen Cove had set her up but not for a date. She had plenty of pairs of jeans and a mountain of cotton shirts, but there wasn't a dress in the mix. This wouldn't do.

She grabbed her hairbrush, her mascara, and her lip

gloss and walked over to Abby's. Hopefully, she'd have something Trinity could borrow. They were about the same build; only Trinity was taller.

The field of grass swayed on the breeze as she moved toward the cabin. The hard rain the day before cleansed the landscape, and the flowers appeared more vibrant. The dirt was a darker brown, and the sky a blue only described in books or seen in touched-up pictures.

Her boots thumped across the porch. She stopped at the door and raised her hand to knock, but Abby swung it open.

"It's about time you came for a visit."

"I've been busy."

"To what do I owe the honor? You miss my tea or maybe the honey?"

She hung her head. She felt bad because she hadn't come to visit Abby, and she'd been on the ranch for weeks. Maybe it was because of her brother.

"Out of sight, out of mind? You know ... Cade isn't a big fan of mine."

Abby stepped to the side and waved her in. "Not true. Cade loves you. He's told me several times."

"Love and trust are two different beasts."

"Tea?"

Trinity looked at her phone. She had an hour before her date, which gave her plenty of time for tea.

"Tea sounds great."

"I heard you're not working at the Brewhouse any longer."

"News travels fast." She sighed. "I was a terrible server, but that's not why I left." She looked over her shoulder, halfway expecting to see Cade.

"He's not here. He went to Lloyd's with Tom to pick up more cattle."

She nodded. "Right."

Abby boiled water in an electric kettle. Within minutes, it was hot. She pulled out pretty teacups and saucers and set a honeypot on the old kitchen table. It was the type that would have made an old-time settler's wife proud with its delicate spindle backs and turned legs. She was surprised the chairs hadn't crumbled under her brother's weight.

She fixed her tea and made it twice as sweet as usual, knowing she had to address a bitter subject.

"There were some men getting handsy with me. Wyatt was there and came to my defense." She could see it that way now, but in the moment all she saw was a man being a problem.

"That's what Cannon told your brother."

Trinity knew it wouldn't take long for word to get back to him. "I'm sure he thinks I started it."

Abby shook her head. "No, I don't think so. The only thing Cade wants is to get his ranch established. A fight at the local bar doesn't influence that, but one here might."

Trinity stared into the amber-colored liquid. "I stay in my room all night so there are no problems. I was never the problem. What is it with guys who think they have a right to touch? I'm not a puppy, or a kitten, or a stuffed animal on a shelf to be rubbed and fondled."

"Men are imbeciles." Abby raised her cup like a beer for a toast. "Here's to strong women and the stupid men we love."

She'd come over with a single purpose. She needed a dress. Asking for one would open up a conversation about her date. She didn't want to go there, but she also wanted to pretty up.

"I was hoping you'd have a dress I could borrow." She gnawed on her upper lip. "I have a date."

"With Wyatt?"

She narrowed her eyes, forcing a notch between her brows. "How did you know?"

"I'm not blind. I've seen you two walking at night. Sometimes you hold hands. Sometimes you giggle and sneak a kiss like a kid. The sound moves through the valley like a megaphone."

"Does my brother know?"

She shrugged. "Not sure. Why would it matter?"

"Because he was serious when he told me not to date anyone who worked for him."

"You're safe then. Wyatt doesn't work for him."

"It's the only reason I said yes." She looked down at her jeans and boots. "The biggest problem is I arrived with one outfit. The people in town were kind enough to give me clothes, but I have nothing to wear on a date."

"I've got some dresses. They come to my knees, so they should cover your bottom."

"That's a priority if I don't want to start another fight."

Abby stood and held out her hand. "Some girls have all the luck. No man has ever fought over me."

Trinity rolled her eyes. "It's way overrated. No one's killed a bear for me."

"That was pretty awesome." Abby giggled all the way to her room.

Like the rest of the cabin, it was built with stacked logs. The warm honey-colored wood had a hand-waxed shine. She wondered if Abby used beeswax to get that glow. Even the bed was made from logs. A patchwork quilt softened the hardness of its sturdy frame.

"I've got yellow, pink, or lavender. What's your preference?"

"I love purple, so let's try that." She expected a *Little House on the Prairie* dress with flounces and lace. Instead, she got a sleeveless sundress with a bold yellow and white floral pattern on a soft purple background.

Abby gave it to her and pointed to the bathroom. "Come out so I can see it."

Trinity changed into the dress and put her boots back on. No matter what she wore, it would be paired with boots since they were all she had.

The skirt of the dress fell to within a few inches of her knees. It was pretty and felt good against her skin. When she walked out to show Abby, she blushed. She'd never had a girlfriend to give her advice about anything.

"What do you think?"

"I think you have the greatest legs in Colorado. Geez, girl, isn't there anything wrong with you?"

She nodded her head enthusiastically, then leaned over to show off the scar on her shoulder. "Horse bite. Needed twenty stitches."

"You say that like you're proud."

"I am. I didn't cry once when Mr. McKinley sewed me up. There was no way I'd ever let a man see me cry."

Abby shook her head. "It's okay to be vulnerable. It's okay to cry."

"Oh, I am vulnerable, and I do cry, but I do it alone."

Abby rushed over and hugged her. "You don't have to be alone, Trinity. You're family."

"True, but cowboy families are different. They live by the cowboy's creed.

Live each day with courage.
Take Pride in your work.
Always finish what you start.
Do what needs to be done.
Be tough, but fair.
Keep your promises.
Stay loyal.
Talk less and say more.
Know where to draw the line."

"You memorized that?"

"It's a religion of sorts." She smiled. "It's also why I knew I could come to Cade. He may not like me, but he loves me, and he's loyal."

Abby took a necklace from her drawer. "Wear this too. It's perfect for the dress."

At the end of a silver chain hung a purple flower.

"Are you sure? What if I lose it?"

"It was five bucks at the dry goods store."

"What happened to that place? I went there looking for underwear, but it was closed."

Abby looked aghast. "Don't tell me you don't have underwear."

Trinity lifted the skirt to show pink cotton hipsters. "I bought these before I lost my job. I earned a few bucks helping Lloyd with a horse too."

She covered her mouth. "Oh. My. God. We promised to feed you if you took care of the horses. I'm so sorry." She looked at her like she'd break.

"I'm fed. Usually, Wyatt cooks, but when he doesn't, I work it out. He buys stuff and hasn't minded sharing yet."

"I'm awful. I promise to stock you guys up this week."

Trinity didn't mind much. She knew what hunger felt

like. It wasn't having Wyatt panfry burgers or bake a chicken. Between them, a chicken could last three days.

"How do I look?"

"Like you're going on a date. Do you need anything else like perfume or makeup? I've got a boatload of it."

She looked at Abby's clear face and couldn't recall ever seeing her wear makeup. "Why would you have a boatload?"

She frowned. "I met your brother's ex. She wore lots of it, and I thought if I dolled myself up, your brother might find me more attractive."

Trinity laughed. "Angie isn't attractive. She's all sizzle and no steak."

Abby looked her over. "You've got the sizzle and the steak."

"With a little mascara and lip gloss, I think I'll do." She smoothed the dress over her thighs. "Thanks for this. Your kindness means a lot." She walked out of the room and down the hallway. "I should be going."

"No, you don't. If this is a date, he can pick you up here."

Trinity smiled. "You're right." This was the stuff she missed by living with men. She texted Wyatt and told him where she'd be when he was ready.

While she waited, she put on the finishing touches and returned to the table for another cup of tea.

She no sooner sat down when a knock sounded at the door.

She jumped up, but Abby shook her head. "I'll get it. Let's make him wait a few seconds. It builds the excitement. Besides, he doesn't need to see how eager you are."

"But I am eager. Do you know how long it's been

since I've been on a real date that didn't happen after several beers and a late night?"

"Someone who looks like you? I'd guess about two weeks."

She shook her head. "Sixteen years old. We went to the county fair, and I bloodied his nose when he tried to cop a feel on the Ferris wheel."

The second knock was louder. "No bloody noses tonight. Whatever happens, is up to you." Abby walked to the door.

A thousand butterflies swarmed Trinity's stomach. She'd only considered the date, not where it would lead to. If it ended with him in her bed, she was okay with that. He'd treated her better than any man prior. Good behavior should be rewarded.

Abby opened the door. "Evening, Wyatt."

"Abby." He nodded and tipped his hat. There was something old fashioned and respectable when a cowboy took off his hat to greet a woman. Not many did these days, but then again, most cowboys were posers and not the real deal. Wyatt was authentic.

"Would you like to come in for a beer or a coffee?"

He looked past her to Trinity. His smile said everything his words hadn't had a chance to. He liked what he saw.

"No ma'am. I've made reservations at Trevi's."

Abby turned and winked at Trinity. "How fancy."

Trinity walked over to him and kissed his cheek. He was dressed all in black from his boots to his hat. This wasn't his regular wear. This was the cowboy equivalent of a tuxedo.

"I'm ready." She looked at Abby. "Thanks for everything."

Abby stood in the doorway after they walked out. "You kids have fun."

When they got to Wyatt's truck, he opened the door and helped her inside. Before he closed it, he leaned in and whispered in her ear, "You made my heart stop tonight."

She smiled all the way to Copper Creek.

When they arrived at the steakhouse, Wyatt exited and rushed around to get her door. It was charming the way he treated her like something special.

At a table by a window, where the sun set before them, they dined and drank wine. She learned a lot about him. He shared how he'd been a city boy with a country heart. He'd walked onto his first ranch and wouldn't leave until they gave him a job. He was eighteen. They shared their deepest fears. His was never amounting to more than a hired hand. Hers was never belonging.

"What do you want to be when you grow up?" she asked.

He smiled. It was a smile that made her heart want so much more.

"I've always wanted to be the foreman. To lead instead of being led." He twirled his wine glass and watched the red liquid fall from the sides. "Lloyd brought in a new guy."

She saw the hurt in his eyes. It would be something if Wyatt was unskilled, but he wasn't. He moved cattle like others moved cars. It was a smooth transition from pasture to pasture. She was called a horse whisperer, but Wyatt was the same with cattle.

"Do you think he's going to replace you?"

He shook his head. "I don't know. I can't live at the ranch, so that makes me less valuable."

"And this other guy can?"

He reached across the table and held her hand. "He's old and grizzled and doesn't pose a threat to Dawson's girls."

She huffed. "Neither do you. Do I need to come over every day and kiss you in front of someone?"

He beamed. "Would you?"

"If you thought it would help."

"God, Three. You sure do make a shit day turn into gold."

She considered her next question. It was one she asked every man she felt something for. How he answered would define the future.

"Why do you like me?" She waited for the canned answer. The one that would get him a failing grade. If the first thing out of his mouth was *because you're pretty*, she'd go home and climb into her bed. If he said anything else, she'd go to the bunkhouse and climb into his.

He stared at her for a long minute. "There are many reasons why I like you. The first is probably because you're not like anyone I've ever met."

Her heart leaped in her chest. "What else?"

"You're smart and funny and stubborn. You make awful oatmeal, but you're thoughtful. I could go on forever and tell you all the things I find charming and frustrating. You can't have one without the other. You're the raisin in my muffin."

She scrunched her nose. "I hate raisins."

"But I love them."

Her breath caught. Was that his way of telling her he loved her? Was it possible to love someone without lying with them? In her experience, words of love and affection only slipped out breathless and sweaty between the sheets. The morning after, everyone forgot they'd been spoken.

When the waitress picked up their plates and asked if they wanted dessert, Trinity looked at Wyatt. "Do you want cake here or something sweeter at home?"

CHAPTER SIXTEEN

Wyatt paid the bill.

"You know, you don't have to offer your sweets because I took you to dinner." He didn't let go of her hand because touching her, however innocent, was almost enough—almost.

"I didn't offer because you took me to dinner. I'm worth far more than steak and wine."

"Yes, you are. Far more than I can afford or hope to deserve."

He walked her to his truck. At the door, he leaned in and took her mouth in a leisurely kiss. The kind of kiss that sent his nerve endings pulsing through his body.

"Please tell me kissing isn't the only thing you can do with those lips."

He stood back and smiled. "I'm going to devour you." He loved a woman who knew what she wanted. Although Trinity didn't complain much about her lot in life, he could see that she had a good feel for what made her happy. He was hoping his lips and tongue were part of the equation.

He couldn't offer her a house with a picket fence, but he could give her hours of languid strokes.

"I'm happy to show you." He opened the door and helped her inside.

They held hands on the way back home. It wasn't late, but it was dark when they arrived. They both stared at Tom's truck.

"Is this going to be a problem for you?" he asked.

She shook her head. "You're not a problem for me. He's not a problem for me."

"He used to be."

She leaned into his shoulder. "I've learned a lot lately. There are some battles worth fighting, and some that aren't. People are assholes, and that fact isn't going away. The only person I can control is me. I make my decisions, and I live with them."

"You're right. Let's go inside and make some good decisions."

When they entered the cabin, it was dark. He took her to his room and closed the door.

"Have I told you how beautiful you look tonight?" He guided her to sit on the edge of his bed, and he dropped to his knees. "You have amazing legs."

"Hours in the saddle."

Dirty thoughts of her riding him for hours floated through his mind, but he kept them to himself. Instead, he ran his hands from the top of her boots to the hem of her skirt. "So soft."

"It's a good thing Abby wears her dresses below her knees."

"You borrowed this dress?" He rested his hands on her thighs. He hated that she had so little. "What happened to your clothes? Surely, in Texas, you had more than a single outfit."

She flopped back on the bedspread. "I did. I had drawers full of clothes, but Blain Wallaby pissed me off."

"Men seem to do that a lot with you. I hope I never end up on your bad side."

"You were when you got me fired."

He took off his boots and lay on the bed beside her. "I didn't get you fired. You quit."

She rolled to her side and stared into his eyes. "You're right, but my firing was inevitable. Better to choose for myself than let someone else take my choice away."

"What made you leave everything in Texas?"

"Do you want to talk about that or do something else?"

He wanted the something else, but he was falling in love with Three, and knowing more about her was as appealing as getting naked. That was a lie, but it was more important than getting naked. Because she was a pretty woman, men rarely looked past the surface. He'd learned a few things over the years. A woman's intelligence couldn't be gauged by her cup size. Someone to talk with was far more entertaining than an easy lay. At the end of the day, it wasn't outer beauty that kept love alive. It was the deep inner beauty that showed in a person's soul.

"I want to know you." He laid a flat palm between her breasts. "What's in here. It's easy to fall in love with the outside of a person. It's not complex. That part is pure attraction, but here." He pressed against her chest above her heart. "This is where the good stuff is."

She smiled and cupped his face. "I don't think anyone has ever said something like that to me."

He laughed. "You said it earlier. Men are assholes.

Most. Not all. I can be, but I want to be something better. For you, I want to be more."

She leaned forward and brushed her lips over his. "Be careful, Mr. Morrison, you almost sound like you're in love."

He put his hand on her hip and tugged her close to him. "I am. Now let me love all of you. Give me your thoughts as well as your body."

He tugged the hem of the dress up to her hips and caressed the soft skin of her thighs. "Tell me everything."

She let out a breath. "My horse died. Blain gave me a horse, but when he let me go, he told me I could only leave with what I arrived with. Given that most of the clothes in my drawers were gifts or things I'd gotten while I was there, I left them behind. It was childish and immature. At my age, I should be past that, but sometimes my inner child lashes out. This time my temper tantrum left me with only the clothes on my back. If Trigger hadn't been a fortune teller and seen that Wallaby Ranch wasn't a long-term solution, I would have hitchhiked instead of driven. Divine intervention got me here in my old SUV. That and the love of an old man who'd seen far too many women come and go."

"I'm so glad you came here. Everything about you makes my life better." He reached behind her and unzipped her dress. "How about that dessert?"

She shifted, and her boots hit the floor one by one. While she unbuttoned his shirt, he tugged at the dress, lifting it over her head and tossing it to the side.

"That's not mine." She squirmed to move away, but he jumped up.

"I've got it." Seconds later, the lavender-colored dress

hung in his closet. She'd undone the buttons of his shirt, so he shrugged it off and tossed it to his dresser.

"Hurry up. I don't want to turn thirty-one while I'm waiting."

She lay there in pink cotton panties and a white bra. There was nothing fancy about any of it, and yet, he'd never seen anything so sexy.

He slowly unbuckled his belt and unbuttoned his jeans. "What's your hurry? We've got all night."

"Do you know how long it's been?" She put her thumbs into the waistband of her underwear, ready to tug them down, but he stopped her with a shake of his head.

"It doesn't matter if it's been a week or a year. I'm not rushing through this. Isn't it time someone gave you something rather than took it?"

He dropped his jeans and boxers. His arousal jutted out like a flag.

"I'm ready for what you have to give me." Her eyes stared at his length.

"In due time. I thought you wanted to know if my tongue's only talent was kissing." He dropped to his knees at the end of the bed and gripped her ankles, tugging, so her bottom hit the edge of the mattress. He started those long languid strokes at her foot and made his way to the soft sensitive area at the inside of her knee.

Each time he hit a ticklish spot, she giggled. It was a sound that filled him with joy. Trinity was a woman who hadn't seen a lot of joy in her life, and her laughter was a gift she didn't give everyone.

He skipped everything in the center of her body and started back at the top of her head.

"Why me, Three? Why do I get to be here with you?" Every man at the restaurant that night wanted her. Some women had that kind of sex appeal. They never fully understood their allure. That was what made them so attractive. Women who flaunted their beauty turned ugly mighty fast.

"Because you see me. Really see me."

"Oh, I do." He moved down her body, reaching underneath her to unfasten her bra. He tossed it aside and stared down at the perfect globes of alabaster skin and rose-colored buds. Sucking one into his mouth pulled a hiss from her. Not one of pain but of pleasure. He licked and laved until she was breathless and squirming. When he was certain she couldn't take any more, he ran his tongue down her stomach until he reached the elastic band of her underwear. Running his thumbs under, he pulled them free and tossed them aside.

For the next hour, he showed her how skilled his tongue could be. He counted the different moans and groans that slipped from her lips. The last one was his favorite sound until the next one came. He nipped, sucked, and pulled until her body shuddered beneath him. He continued until it happened again. When she lay limp on the mattress, he moved on top of her.

"You ready for the good stuff?"

Her eyes looked love drunk. Her skin flushed pink with passion.

"That wasn't the good stuff?" she asked.

"No, baby. We're only getting started." He wrapped up and pressed into her. Hot and velvet and tight as a glove, she hugged on to him like he was the most challenging ride in her life.

He pushed her to the edge multiple times.

He wasn't sixteen. He didn't have the refractory time of a teen, but he had the staying power of a man, and he knew how to please a woman. When he was finished with Trinity, he wanted her to feel like no other man would ever do. *Finished with Trinity … that will never happen.*

One taste of her was enough for him to know, he was an addict, and only she would satisfy his cravings.

"Geez, Wyatt. What the hell are you made of?" She wrapped her long legs around his thighs.

"I'm all heart and steel."

"I feel it. All of it."

He stalled, and every inch of him shook. He was so ready to explode, but his heart needed to know.

He looked beyond her messy blonde hair, and her sex flushed cheeks. Her perfect breasts reaching for his mouth and the tight fist of her throbbing around him, as he stared deep into her soulful eyes.

"Do you think you could ever love a man like me?"

She smiled up at him. "I think I already do."

He pumped into her until her body shuddered, and he released on the echoes of her words. *I think I already do.*

Basking in the afterglow, he wrapped his arms around her and held on tight. Nothing would come between them again. She'd said it right earlier. Some things were worth fighting for, and some weren't. Trinity was worth any fight he'd have to enter.

CHAPTER SEVENTEEN

Could a morning get any better? Trinity rolled into Wyatt's side, seeking out his warmth. Late spring nights dropped into the thirties in the mountains. The only heat in the bunkhouse came from the fireplace, which hadn't been lit since she arrived.

"Is it time to get up already?" His groggy voice whispered in her ear. "It feels like we just fell asleep."

She laughed. "Time to pay the piper." She moved to get up, but Wyatt tugged her back against his nakedness.

"Again?"

He softly bit her shoulder. "I wish we had time, but we have work. Why didn't we choose career fields where we could laze around on the weekend?"

"Because you love cattle, and I love horses." *And you.* "I'll make the coffee if you get the shower started. We can conserve time and water by bathing together."

"I like the way you think even though it's faulty because I plan to be thorough when lathering you up."

She climbed out of bed and rooted around in the dark

for her clothes before she remembered he'd hung up Abby's dress.

Wyatt flipped on the light switch and stared at her. "Any way I can keep you locked in my room naked?"

Her heart hitched. He wanted to keep her. Naked, but still keep her.

"That sounds kind of nice, but I've got to earn my keep, and horses kept in stables don't feed themselves."

She moved to his closet and tugged one of his plaid flannels from a hanger. She put it on and buttoned it up. Wyatt was tall, but so was she. Even so, the hem reached just above her knees.

"It would be worth taking over your chores just to keep you here." He tugged on his jeans and walked up behind her, nuzzling her neck.

She opened the door and they walked out together. Wyatt pushed against her backside, nibbling the crook of her neck at the spot that brought a giggle to her lips.

Tom exited his room and looked past her to Wyatt. "Riding her must be about as exciting as mounting a state fair pony."

Wyatt took a threatening step toward Tom, but she gripped his arm. "Let it go."

Tom brushed past them on his way to the kitchen.

"Why do you let him talk about you like that?"

She turned around so she could see Wyatt's face. "Tom is a lit match. Tossing gas or dry paper on him is stupid. I'm not stupid."

"No, you're not." He kissed her forehead. "I'll make the coffee. You start the shower. I'll be there in a few minutes."

She shook her head. "No way. You're not going out there. I've seen you in action when you get jealous. Not a pretty sight." She slid a finger through his belt loop. "We'll shower and then deal with the coffee if Tom hasn't already brewed it."

On most occasions, showering as a couple would lead to all kinds of fun, but they had work to do, so the time was relegated to actually getting clean rather than getting dirty.

They separated at their doors to dress.

Five minutes later, she kissed Wyatt in front of the coffee pot and told him she needed to feed the horses, and she'd meet him at his truck in fifteen minutes.

Scamp moved to the edge of her stall.

"Sorry, sweetheart. I'm not riding with you today." She stroked the horse's muzzle. "I'm hanging out with my boyfriend." Warmth filled her. It was the first real relationship she'd had in her adult life. The first time she felt more than a liking for a man. He was the birthday cake she never got. The present under the tree that never arrived. The man was a damn unicorn. Maybe it wasn't never belonging somewhere that she feared. It was never belonging to someone. Now that she'd gotten a taste of what love felt like, she wasn't willing to give it up.

She made sure Scamp had fresh water and hay and then skipped out of the barn to find Cade talking to Wyatt. She approached warily. Had Abby said something to him? Was he warning Wyatt against her? There were a thousand thoughts that went through her mind, but when she approached and saw her brother's smile, she let them go.

"Hey, Trin." He looked between her and Wyatt. "I was just telling Wyatt that he's been loaned out to the Mosier Ranch."

She saw the look in Wyatt's eyes. He was hurt that

he'd been pushed away from the Big D. It wasn't that he didn't expect the change. With the presence of the old man he described, it was a given, but it didn't soften the blow.

"On loan? This is temporary?" Her heart stopped for a beat.

"Not sure. For now, Wyatt is an employee of Mosier Ranch. I thought maybe you could help him bring his horses back and get them settled into the stable. Maybe even take him on an official tour of the property."

She opened her mouth, but no words came out. Instead, she nodded and walked to Wyatt's truck. To stand there would be like rubbing salt in a wound. Wyatt was now an employee of her brother's, so that meant he was off-limits.

Why was life so cruel? It gave her a taste of something amazing and then snatched it away.

When Wyatt entered the truck, he took her hand. "We'll work it out."

She shook her head. "There's nothing to work out. I made a promise, and a person is only as good as their word."

He put the truck in gear and headed for the Big D.

"That's bullshit. I just got you. I'm not ready to give you up."

It was a personal policy to never let a man see her cry. She turned to the window and let the tears fall silently down her cheeks.

By the time they arrived at Lloyd's, she'd gotten herself under control.

"You hook up the trailer, and I'll get the horses ready."

He leaned over, but she exited the truck before he could touch her. To feel his touch on her skin would only make her want him more. At least she had the memories of last night.

Wyatt backed the trailer close to the stables.

Lloyd walked down from the main house. He handed a check to Wyatt.

To Trinity, it was eerily reminiscent of her last day on Wallaby Ranch.

"Wyatt, you've been an amazing help. With Jimmy coming on board and Cade needing another hand, I thought it best to share you."

She tugged Rex toward the trailer. Listening to Lloyd made her angry. He treated Wyatt like he had little value.

"Thank you, sir. Working on the Big D has been a pleasure."

The word loan was inaccurate. He wasn't being loaned to anyone. He was being given to Cade. He had two choices: he could settle in at Cade's ranch or find someplace else.

She got Rex secure and went to get Red. He saw the trailer and rose up on his hind legs.

Wyatt ran over to help, but she held up a hand.

"I've got him. He's scared. You get the tack."

She moved the horse away from the trailer and talked softly to him. "Hey, boy. I know you're scared. You've done this before. We're all in for a change." She remembered an old hand at McKinley ranch used to say that *change was a challenge and an opportunity, not a threat.* This change threatened everything.

Her phone beeped with an incoming message which startled Red again. She tied him to the fencepost to give him a chance to calm down.

When she looked at her phone, she laughed. "You're

right. I was wrong. When can you get back to Texas? Angel's horse needs you."

She glanced up to the sky. "Is this a damn test?"

"Is what a test?"

"Just got a text from my old boss asking me to come back." She untied Red and led him to the trailer. This time she cooed to him until he was inside and secure.

Wyatt leaned on the side of the trailer, waiting for her. "You're not going, are you?"

She rubbed her hand over her face. "It would make it easier on everyone."

He moved toward her and pulled her close. Their noses touched as he spoke. "Please don't go. I'll work it out with your brother. I'll find another job. Hell, I'll wait tables at the Brewhouse if it means I can be with you."

She laughed. "You'd probably be better at it."

He kissed her gently. "Don't leave. We've only just begun."

She leaned into him and breathed in his scent. The lavender of his fabric softener was supposed to be calming, but Wyatt did nothing to slow her heart rate. His was the scent that made it race when he kissed her. He was the everything she needed but couldn't have.

She looked at the darkening sky. "We should go if you want to ride the fence."

He smirked. "I'd rather ride something else."

She let out a sigh of resignation. "Me too, but those days are over."

He shook his head. "We had one day, and it wasn't enough. We can work around it."

She raised her hands in surrender. "Cade's rules, not mine."

154

"He changed the rules after the players were already in play. He's going to have to change his position."

She closed the trailer and climbed into the truck.

When Wyatt took his place behind the steering wheel, she turned to look at him.

"This isn't a game, Wyatt."

He leaned over and cupped the back of her head, pulling her in. When his lips touched hers, he said, "This is a war I intend to win."

———

THE HORSES WERE easy to unload. Red was as docile as a goldfish when she backed him out and led him into the stables. There weren't a lot of stalls like they had at Lloyd's but enough to house eight horses. With the addition of Rex and Red, there were now five. At least she'd have stuff to do daily.

She chose the stall next to her brother's horses. It was childish, but she didn't want Wyatt's animals close to Tom's.

She felt sorry for his mare. Willow didn't get to choose her owner, but if she had, Trinity was certain it wouldn't have been him.

She saddled Red while Wyatt saddled Rex. Tom arrived at the same time. He removed his horse's equipment and shoved her into the stall before he made for the door.

"Wait a minute. You need to brush her down and feed and water her." She'd noticed the small sores on Willow's back. Sores that only came with laziness and neglect. She'd even applied salve to them in hopes that she could get the irritation to go away. The problem was Tom, and he wasn't going anywhere.

"Seems to me that's your job." He walked off and left them in the stable.

With a growl, Trinity handed Wyatt the reins and told him she'd be a few minutes.

She brushed the salt off Willow's coat before she fed and watered her. It seemed as if every female Tom came into contact with, whether horse or human, suffered.

CHAPTER EIGHTEEN

Wyatt waited outside the stables while Three took care of Willow. They were a good team in a bad spot. He considered taking her away. Neither were happy with their current situation. It wasn't that he didn't want to work for Cade. He liked the man, but he didn't like Tom. Tom might be good with cattle, but he was awful with everything else.

He'd have to talk to her about it. He didn't know where they'd go, but anywhere together was better than being here without her.

She walked out looking like an angry ruler with her back straight and stiff, and her forehead lined with concern.

"That horse deserves better. Poor thing has so many hotspots from neglect. I'm surprised she allows him to climb on her back."

"You ready to go?" He handed her Red's reins and waited for her to mount him. He was a big horse, but Three was limber and strong and swung herself on his back with ease. "Show me the property."

"I'm sure you've already seen most of it. You live here."

He chuckled. "I have, but I haven't seen it with you, and that makes the experience different. Ever notice that you can view things differently if you're looking at them through a different lens? Show me this ranch through your eyes."

"Let's ride the fence. It'll take hours, which will keep me away from Tom and save his life." She shook the reins and led the way.

They rode in silence for the first hour. There was nothing awkward about the quiet—it was comfortable with Three—but he wanted to know more about her.

"If you could be anywhere, where would you go?" he asked.

She slowed down so he could catch up and ride alongside her.

"My perfect place isn't a place but a feeling. I had it once at the Mercers' ranch. I was part of a larger family. Not necessarily a family by blood but by something stronger and deeper. We were a family by choice. It seemed that once we left Colorado, my choices were made by others." She frowned and shook her head. "That's not really true. I make the choice to stay silent and suck it up. I do that because if I really let loose ... that storm my brother describes me as would destroy everything in its path. Right now, I'm a leaf in my own wind."

He reached over and took her hand. "I love your wind. Let it blow, baby; you can't keep suppressing your rage. It tears you up inside."

She dropped his hand and laughed. "Better to tear me up than everyone around me." She turned where the fence angled right. "Didn't you help put this fence up?"

He nodded. "Some of it. Lloyd jumped the gun and delivered a bunch of cattle before your brother was ready. That got him into hot water with Abby." He turned to look at the cabin that was just a dot on the landscape. "She blamed his cows for knocking over her hives and then accidentally started a fire to the section of land between her place and the bunkhouse. Lloyd felt bad and volunteered Baz and me and himself to put up the fence between the properties."

"Geez, you'd think, as his sister, I'd hear about these things."

"Your brother is an island. Or he was until he met Abby. I'd say give him some time to adjust to her. People in relationships tend to be more open. Like us. You should be more open with me about the things that hurt you."

She stopped the horse and looked his way. "Don't you get it? We can't be together any longer."

"Then we'll leave because I'm not living without you now that I've got you."

She narrowed her eyes. "You've got me? I'm not a possession."

"Come on, Trinity, you know what I mean. We're together. Let me put it this way. You have me, and I don't want to belong or be with anyone else. If that means we leave the ranch and find another way, then that's okay too."

"No, it's not. You told me you wanted to be a foreman of a ranch. Let me tell you ... this is your best chance." She swung out her hand as if revealing a prize.

"I'm low man again. If anyone is in charge, it's Tom."

"Tom is an idiot. He's really great at disguising his stupidity. Fabulous at being a chameleon, so he blends in, but you and I both know he's an asshat. Eventually, he'll show himself. My brother may be blind, but he isn't stupid. Tom may fool him for a while but not long-term. You'll get your chance, and you'll be fabulous." She gave Red a kick and bolted forward.

The conversation was finished, for now. He galloped behind her. Watching her hair blow in the wind and the joy flowing from her body when she rode told him she needed to be right where she was. She belonged on that horse at this ranch. Despite the gray cloud cover and the prickling of the storm's energy in the air, she was like sunshine.

The first crack of lightning and boom of thunder startled Red. He reared up, and Wyatt's heart halted, thinking Three was about to take a tumble, but she calmed him with her voice and her demeanor. She always appeared unflappable, but inside she had to be trembling.

Next came the rain. It wasn't a problem beyond discomfort.

"Which is closer, the shelter or the cabin?" he asked.

She looked ahead of her and then behind her. "I'd say the shelter." She gave Red a tap with her boot and pushed forward into the storm. As the shelter came into view, tiny hail rained down on them.

"When we get there, don't unsaddle him. Let the saddle protect him and let him run," he yelled.

The hailstones grew from pea size to dimes, and their hits stung his skin.

Three reached the shelter before him. She dismounted and slapped Red's hind end to get him moving for cover. There wasn't much available, but in his experience, animals were pretty self-sufficient. At least they were self-preserving.

He caught up and did the same, then tugged Three

into the shelter. It wasn't anything special. Just a box with a cot, a table, and a few days of supplies.

"You helped deliver this too?"

"I did, but I couldn't remember where it was on the land." He pulled a towel from a nearby box and tossed it to her.

When she was finished getting what water she could off her body, she handed it back.

"That was chivalrous. Now you have a wet towel to dry off with."

He winked. "I'll survive. Besides ..." He glanced at the cot. "I thought maybe you could warm me up." He toweled off and hung the wet terry cloth from a nail on the wall. He flopped onto the cot and patted the space beside him. "You know ... they say if a person has hypothermia, they should get skin to skin with another person."

She tried to keep a straight face, but the muscles at the corner of her lips won when they lifted.

"You're not hypothermic." She took the space beside him and leaned against the wall.

The *ping ping ding* of hail hitting the roof filled the tiny box with noise. She shivered and moved closer.

"No, but we can make sure neither of us get there. It's important to take precautions."

"Always the boy scout. What's their motto?"

He raised three fingers and said, "Be prepared."

Her shoulders shook with her laughter. "You really were a Scout?"

He scoffed. "Scouting rocked at first. In fact, it's where I learned to ride a horse. Got a merit badge for horsemanship. I quit because there wasn't a cowboy badge." He chuckled. "My mom had her sights set on me being an architect or a lawyer or something like that. She never thought joining Boy Scouts of America would make me a cowboy."

The hail grew heavier, hitting the room like bullets discharged from a gun.

"Why is it they say there's a chance of a storm every day? Can't they get it right? You'd think with all the technology they'd see something like this coming."

He shrugged. "Saying there's a chance protects them."

"You think the horses are okay?"

"They've survived storms for thousands of years. I'm sure they'll live through this one."

She shivered. "It is cold."

He couldn't argue there. They were wet, and the shelter was probably covered in a few inches of hail.

"Let me warm you."

He started with the buttons of her shirt. When he peeled the wet fabric from her skin, he moved to her boots and jeans.

She joined in the undressing and quickly divested him of his shirt and pants. Within minutes they were naked.

"I'm only doing this because I don't want you to get hypothermia."

He gloved up, rose above her, and pressed into her body. "Exactly. Thanks for your care and concern."

"I do care," she said on a groan.

He moved in and out of her with long leisurely strokes. He loved the way her eyes rolled back when he hit the right spot. Loved how her eyelashes fluttered against her cheeks. Loved the sounds she made without thought. When she moaned, it was like getting every good thing he'd ever asked for.

He wasn't a man who wanted much, but he wanted this woman.

"I'm not letting you push me away," he said. "You don't like people making choices for you. Don't make them for me." He thrust inside her and stilled.

Her eyes flew open. He knew they would. He'd touched a raw nerve in her heart.

"You hear me?"

She nodded. "I hear you." She pushed his hips away and then pulled them forward. He rolled over and let her set the pace. He closed his eyes and felt everything from the way she rode him to the way she made him feel. Three made him want to be more than a cowboy. For her, he'd become anything.

When he felt the start of her core fluttering, he gripped her hips and slowed her motion so he could feel every pulse. Seconds later, he followed her to the end.

She lay on his chest while he drew circles on her back. They should have been cold. They weren't.

He was so content that he didn't notice the storm had passed until he heard the neigh of one of the horses.

"I guess that's our signal to get up and get dressed." He patted her bottom and watched her rise. He'd never get tired of looking at her.

She tugged on her wet underwear and jeans.

He tied off the condom and tucked it into the pocket of his pants.

Just as they were pulling on their shirts, the door to the shelter opened, and there stood Cade.

CHAPTER NINETEEN

She looked up to see her brother blocking the doorway.

If the universe was going to kick her while she was down, she wondered why she hadn't gotten hit by a lightning bolt when they were racing through the storm for shelter. It would have been a quicker and less painful way to go.

She tugged her damp shirt to the center to fasten the last button.

"We're okay."

He lifted a brow. "I can see that."

"It's not what you think." Her heart hated the lie. It was exactly what he thought. Sadly, finding her in the shelter with Wyatt, both of them dressing, would only confirm the rumors about her reputation. She'd just proven every lie to be true. How could she say she didn't sleep around when she was caught? "We were wet from the storm. Did you think we'd sit here and get hypothermia?" She gave Wyatt a don't-say-a-word look. Thankfully he didn't.

"Is that true? Were you undressed to dry off?" He stepped inside the room and glanced around.

What did he think, there'd be spent condoms laying everywhere? She snapped her head toward the cot, hoping he hadn't left the one they'd used sitting out in the open. Wyatt tapped his pocket as if he knew exactly what she was thinking.

She released the breath she hadn't known she'd been holding.

"Is it true?" Cade asked again.

Her shoulder rolled forward, and she sighed. "No, it's not true. I mean yes, we took our clothes off to let them dry. It's true, we didn't want to die from hypothermia, but that was our excuse—our justification."

"I warned you, Trinity. No sleeping with the staff."

Wyatt stepped in front of her. "That's not fair. I'm tired of the men at this ranch not giving her the benefit of the doubt."

"If she were a guy, I'd say she was thinking with the wrong head. Ignoring my rules means she's not thinking at all."

She tried to step to the side of him, but he stood in front of her like a shield. Although he was tall and muscular and had broad shoulders and washboard abs, he wasn't as big as her brother.

"She wasn't breaking your rules. I wasn't working for you. I was working for Lloyd. We started this relationship weeks ago."

Cade seemed to grow bigger with each inhale. "Time to end it. Make-ups and break-ups destroy a business. I can't risk losing mine." He turned and walked out of the shelter.

Her knees buckled, and Wyatt caught her. She rarely let her emotions show, but standing there for those few minutes and seeing the judgment in Cade's eyes destroyed her. She had to choose right there. Would it be Cade or Wyatt? One would destroy two lives, the other only hers.

"We can't do this." She wrenched herself free and walked out the door. "I'll get Red back to the stables."

"Trinity," he called after her. It was kind of like being in trouble. When she was in her family's good grace, they called her Trin. When she was in trouble, those three syllables were spat out like darts seeking a target.

Thankfully, Red was munching on grass in the middle of the field. She rushed to him and looked him over. He didn't seem worse for the wear, though she was certain he'd be happy to get the soppy saddle off his back. "Ready to go home, boy?"

She looked over her shoulder to see Wyatt moving toward the fence where Rex stood. She gave the horse a soft nudge and steered him toward home.

All the way, her emotions scraped at her insides to let go. She swallowed so much that her throat hurt. Her eyes bulged with unshed tears, and she raced toward the stables. She needed to talk to someone. Someone who would understand what she was going through. Someone who'd sucked up everyone's negativity and taken all the punches. The only person she knew who'd walked through fire and came out cool on the other side was Goldie. The weeks she'd worked with her were entertaining as she shot her vlog posts and told people to keep it real.

She'd understand how it was to have to be someone she wasn't to survive.

When she reached the stable an hour later, she made

sure to groom Red and check for injury. Short of a few swollen spots on his muzzle, he looked fine. She walked out as Wyatt walked in.

He stopped her. "Please don't shut me out. We can make this work. Your brother doesn't have to know. We can keep this off the ranch."

She shook her head. "I've never been a good liar. Look what I did in the shelter. All I had to do was say yes, it was all about drying the clothes, and he would have accepted it, but I've never been a liar. It's not in my nature to be dishonest or disloyal. Loving you and Cade is a problem for me. I want to be loyal to my feelings for you, but I owe my brother loyalty too. Don't ask me to choose."

She walked away, feeling lower than low. Her biggest complaint in life was that someone always tried to make choices for her. Now she was faced with one of the hardest decisions, and she wished someone else would decide.

She didn't bother going into the bunkhouse to change. She was almost dry anyway. What she needed was wise council. She wasn't sure if she could get it from Goldie, but she'd try.

Knowing her schedule, she bypassed town and drove up the country road to where Tilden and Goldie had built their new home. Like the stable, the Cooper brothers had erected the structure in weeks.

She was no sooner out of her car when Goldie opened the door of the old cabin and waved her inside.

"What are you doing here?"

Trinity took three steps and burst into tears. "I ... I ... I'm a mess." She fell into Goldie's arms and went wherever she was led.

"Let's make some tea. It's really the cure for all ailments. And chocolate. And sex."

At the mention of sex, Trinity wailed louder. "I'm giving it all up." She swiped a napkin from the holder and dabbed at her eyes. "Not the tea. I'll take that."

Goldie opened cupboards and pulled containers down. When she popped the tops, there was a bin of chocolate, one of cookies, and one of hard candy.

"You help yourself while I get the tea."

"I'm not giving up chocolate either, but I'll have to give up sex." She looked around. "You don't have that in a plastic tub, do you?"

Goldie laughed. "No, but I did get sponsored once by a sex toy company." She set two cups on the small table. They weren't dainty and feminine like Abby's but sturdy man cups. "If you're keeping men around just for the sex …" She looked left and right. "There's no need. They've got a device for that. The Womanizer is all a girl needs for satisfaction. Love is something else. If you're crying, it's a pain in the heart that's driving it."

"You're so right. No pain in the ass is worth these tears." She swiped at them again, but they kept rolling down her cheeks. She'd had one big cry since she became an adult. Wasn't she entitled to one a decade?

The kettle whistled, and Goldie gathered tea bags and honey. "This is from Abby. Her bees make the best honey. I bet she sings to them."

A vision of Abby standing in front of her hives singing broke the sorrow and replaced it with a laugh. "I don't know her well enough to say, but she's sweet. She's got a good heart. Hell, she puts up with my brother, and that means she's a damn saint."

"You gonna tell me what happened, or do I need to

put you into a sugar coma and squeeze it out of you?"

Trinity settled back in the chair. It dawned on her that they were in the old house. "Why are you here when you've got that big house next door?"

She held up two fingers. "Two reasons. One is because I love it here. Two is because we're letting a guest stay, and I needed to get it ready."

"A guest?"

She leaned in and whispered. "Yes. You remember that guy who owns the dry goods store?"

Trinity didn't know why, but she remembered his name. "Jake Powers?"

Goldie sat up, and her eyes grew bright. "I knew I recognized him. He's a life coach. You know, the guys that tell you how to be successful and stuff. He's got a huge social media profile. We used to have the same agent before mine canned me. Anyway, since I kind of know him and Tilden got some help from Doc at one time, we're paying back the favor and letting him stay here until he opens the store and moves on."

"Do you know what they're putting in?"

"No, it's like area 51. Top Secret. If they tell you, they'll have to kill you."

It was irrelevant to Trinity. On the way up, she'd thought about her options. A week ago, she would have been stuck, but Blain wanted her back. Her father always said to never cross the same bridge twice, but right now, Blain was the only bridge that could get her away from here.

"I'm sure it will be great. You'll have to text me and let me know when it opens."

She frowned and shook her head. "You can see for yourself." She doctored her tea and picked through the candy to get a chocolate kiss. "You look like you need this."

"I really do."

Trinity spent the next ten minutes telling her everything, and when she was finished, Goldie just stared.

"Your brother is a dolt. Doesn't he know that a well-sexed cowboy is a happy cowboy? That a man who has something at home doesn't spend his nights getting in trouble elsewhere?"

"All my brother is thinking about is his ranch. I can't blame him. His ex-wife did a real number on him. Took everything and put his plan ten years behind schedule. There's merit to his argument."

"But you love Wyatt. That has to mean something."

"It means everything. To me. Not to Cade."

"Don't go back to Texas. That guy you worked for is a bigger idiot than your brother. If Wyatt lets you go, then he's the biggest idiot of all."

She tasted her tea and made a face. It wasn't anything she was used to. "What kind of tea is this?"

Goldie smiled. "It's called Happiness Tea. I read the ingredients, and it has everything from flowers to fruits."

Trinity put another helping of honey into it. "It tastes like dirt."

"I know, right?" She picked up both cups and dumped them into the sink. "Makes you happy to toss it away."

Trinity laughed. "I knew this was the right place to come. You're such a funny person."

She shrugged. "Funny used to pay the bills, and now getting real does."

"Where's Tilden?"

She clapped her hands. "He's fishing with Cannon,

Bowie, and Ben. When he gets back, I'm gutting trout for my fans."

"What if he doesn't catch anything?"

"Then, I'll show them how to gut Tilden."

"You two are so fun together."

"Oh yeah, it was a barrel of laughs at the beginning. He was a dog, and I was a cat. We spent the first few weeks barking and scratching at each other."

"But it worked out."

"It did because I learned that nice trumped everything. I also learned that being honest with myself helped me to be honest with others, and that opened a lot of doors. Maybe you're the flipside. Be honest with others about how they make you feel, and maybe then you can be honest with yourself. I mean, really honest. Are you willing to give up Wyatt because your brother is shortsighted? You're thirty years old."

"It would be different if I wasn't living on his land."

"Tell you what. As soon as Jake Powers leaves, you can live here."

"Really?" Could it be that easy? "I don't make anything living and working at Cade's, so I'll have to get a job."

"Come back to the Brewhouse."

"Oh, Lord no. I was awful."

Goldie laughed. "You were. I was bad, but honey, you were worse. We'll find you something. I learned that in Aspen Cove, anything is possible."

She left Goldie's feeling like things were going to be okay. If she didn't work on her brother's ranch, she couldn't be breaking his rules. All she needed to do was hope for Mr. Powers to finish up his business and move on.

CHAPTER TWENTY

Wyatt waited on the porch for Three. She walked away from him like it was over. It was never going to be over. She had crawled under his skin. She lived in his cells. It wasn't the sex that brought him to this place. He broke the cardinal rule of dating women. He courted her before he dated her and before he slept with her. It was so much easier to walk away when you didn't know the person's heart. He knew her heart, and it was all good.

His first instinct was to beat some sense into her brother. He understood his position. A new ranch didn't need to be rumored to have discontent. He could also understand her brother's distrust of his sister. If the rumors flowed about her, no matter how untrue, it wouldn't take many repeats to put doubt in anyone's mind. But Three was Cade's sister. She had been raised on the same values.

Wyatt rubbed his jaw and growled.

In the distance, a cloud of dirt kicked up with the arrival of someone tearing down the unpaved road. His hope of it being Three was dashed when a blue truck arrived.

Tom pushed the door open and climbed out.

"Are you pining for your lost love?" He slammed the door shut and walked toward the bunkhouse.

"Why are you such an asshole to her?"

He walked up the steps and leaned against the railing. "She's been an asshole to me since the day I met her. What did big brother think when he found you naked in the shelter?"

"Wait ... how did you know?"

Tom laughed. "It was a good guess. Put Trinity near a mattress, and she'll lay flat on her back every time."

Wyatt lunged toward Tom. "Your problem is she would never spread her legs for you."

Tom stood his ground. "And you think you're special? She is what she is, and now her brother knows it for sure."

Wyatt pushed against Tom, nearly toppling him backward over the rail. "You told her brother to check on us."

"Just being neighborly. The hail was large, and you two were gone for a while. How was I supposed to know?"

Wyatt threw the first punch, and it was a doozy. Tom's head snapped back, knocking his Stetson off and sending him over the rail. He hit the ground but popped up like a pugilist ready for the next round.

Not wanting Tom to have to put himself out, Wyatt jumped the rail and landed in front of him, fists at the ready. He was prepared to take a hit or two but wasn't prepared for the velocity at which it struck. He reached out and grasped Tom's collar before he stumbled back. The collar tore free, leaving a strip of plaid in his hand.

He used it to wipe the blood from his nose and tossed it to the ground.

"This one is for Trinity," he yelled as he threw the punch and connected with Tom's jaw.

The man took a step back and regrouped to charge forward. Wyatt wound up in a bear hug rolling on the ground.

Their fight must have been loud because the next thing he knew, Tom was pulled off him, and Cade stood between them.

"What the hell is going on here?"

Wyatt stepped back and dusted off his jeans. "He started it."

Tom picked his Stetson up and shoved it on his head. "You threw the first punch."

Cade looked between them. "Is that the truth?"

He'd seen what the truth did for Three—nothing. He bent it. "His mouth fired first."

"Don't tell me this is about my sister."

"This isn't about Three."

"Who?" Tom and Cade said simultaneously.

"I'm talking about Trinity. You know, bold, ballsy, and beautiful in heart and soul. This fight isn't about Trinity. It's about choices." He turned to Cade. "You're choosing this asshole over your sister. Maybe you should listen to her. You said this afternoon that if she were a man, you'd accuse her of thinking with the wrong head. All I'm saying is open your eyes, man. Take your eyes off your ranch and cattle for a second, and see what's really happening." He marched past Cade and threw another punch, hitting Tom directly in the nose. "That one's for me."

He turned and faced Cade. "If you want me gone, I'll pack up and leave now."

Cade threw up his hands. "What I want is for you two to figure out a way to work together. If you can't, I'll replace both of you."

Wyatt turned on his boots and walked into the bunkhouse. He would have thrown his shit in his truck and left if it wasn't for Three. He'd hoped to see her before he fell asleep, but the hot shower and the fight had taken the last of his energy. When his head hit the pillow, he was out.

When he woke, he went to her door, but it was locked. He tapped lightly but got no answer.

"We're not done, Three. We'll never be done."

CHAPTER TWENTY-ONE

The hardest thing to do was not open the door when Wyatt knocked. She was lying there, awake. She had already been out to muck the stalls and feed the horses. Avoiding him was the only way to survive being around him. Everything about him attracted her. He was metal. She was a magnet.

When she entered the kitchen area, she found a full coffee pot made with double the grounds the way she liked it. A note was stuck to a mug left on the counter.

Three,

Let me take you to dinner. I think we can work it out. We belong together.

Love, Wyatt

She hugged the note to her chest. They could work it out. All she needed to do was leave the ranch, but until she could find a job elsewhere and a place to live, she'd have to stay here, and they'd have to stay apart. She'd made a promise to her brother, and that was binding in her mind.

When she stepped onto the porch with a coffee

clutched in her hand, she saw Cade riding toward her. His hard expression would scare the average person, but Trinity was used to the gruff cowboy demeanor all the Mosiers adopted. In reality, they were impenetrable steel on the surface, but once you got past the hardness, they were soft and sweet like kittens or puppies.

He rode Scamp to within feet of the porch before he dropped to the dirt.

She acknowledged his presence with a lift of her chin.

"I left Wyatt to fence off pasture one. We're dividing up the land for efficiency."

She stared at him, not knowing why he was sharing the information. Currently, he had a big fence surrounding the property but little division in between. Maybe a fence that split the land in two. After seeing Lloyd's setup, it made sense to further divide it.

"Okay. And this matters to me because?"

"It doesn't, except to stay away from pasture one. I would have put Tom and Wyatt on it together, but after their fight last night, I didn't think it was wise to put tools in their hands that could be used as weapons."

She knew her expression was one of shock because that's what she felt. "They fought?"

"Come on, Trinity. It's the same as always. Men fight, and somehow you're in the middle of it."

Indignance straightened her spine.

"I wasn't even here. I went to Goldie's, and then into Copper Creek to get some cash. A girl needs things like tampons and deodorant. Don't blame what they did on me."

He shook his head. "Like I said when you showed up, you may not cause the trouble, but it follows you."

"Why is it I have to take the blame? If they fought, it

was because Tom was being a bastard. What do you see in that guy?" She raised her hands. "Why him?"

"He was available, and I could afford him. I can't be picky while my budget is tight."

"Yeah, well, you get what you pay for. He may be able to ride a horse or fix a fence, but part of the worth of a man is the content of his character, and Tom is morally bankrupt." Thinking about the guy made her mad. "Have you seen his horse? He doesn't even brush her down. He rides in and tosses his saddle aside then leaves her salty and sweaty. She's got abscesses all over her back. The poor thing has so many scars. Those are the ones you can see. Imagine what she's got inside. That poor horse has been abused her whole life."

The burn inside her grew hotter. "Imagine being punished all the time because those in charge don't take the time to really pay attention." She let out a sound that was part sigh and part growl. "I give her extra care because, after years of neglect, she's probably used to her lot in life, but I want her to know she has value. She's important. She deserves better."

Cade looked at her sideways. "Are we still talking about the horse?"

She stomped her boot. "Of course, we're talking about the horse."

"Mm-hmm." He shook his head like there was a fly in his ear. "All I stopped by to say was this thing with Wyatt can't happen. I want the reputation of a good rancher, and I can't get that if my ranch hands are fighting over my sister." He waved his hand around. "I know, you said it wasn't about you, but you and I both know it was. Wyatt has a ripe apple on his cheek, and Tom is sporting two black eyes."

Inside, a happy dance was in full force because Tom had gotten his ass kicked. If Wyatt had a swollen cheek, then he deserved that too. Especially if he'd fought the idiot over her. The men in her life should know she had a very long fuse, but once the fire hit the dynamite, God help them. At this point, her fuse was burning danger-ously close to the wick, and an explosion was inevitable.

"I don't need people to throw fists for me." She leaned forward. Standing on the porch, she was inches taller than Cade. "What I need and have always needed is someone to have my back. It's really too bad the only person willing to step up, is a man I'm not allowed to like."

Cade took off his hat and ran his hand through his hair. "It never works, Trin. Remember, don't mix mattresses and money."

She looked to the side to see Abby's cabin. "Tell that to your woman." She tossed the cold coffee left in the bottom of her cup to the ground. "Anything else you need?"

He pressed his hat on his head. "No. Contrary to your belief, I do have your back. It's why you're living here. In a way, I'm protecting you by demanding you stay away from Wyatt."

"No, big brother. You're protecting yourself. If you truly had my back, you'd be happy I found someone I could love."

"It would never work. Workplace romances rarely do and then what?" He looked to the sky. "Weatherman says it could storm again today."

"That's what they say every day." She turned to leave but stopped. "Can I take Sable for a ride? She's getting antsy. I know Abby usually rides her when you two tour the property, but you've been busy." It was her way of telling him not to neglect everything. She was his sister, so it's not like she could change that, but Abby didn't have to put up with him.

His eyes grew concerned. "Did my Beeleesi say something to you?"

"Beeleesi?" She found it charming that her brother had also chosen a nickname for the one he loved. Too bad he was the only one allowed to love on the ranch. His ranch. His rules.

He blushed. "I know it's silly, but she's the queen of bees." He narrowed his eyes. "Seriously, Trin, did she say she was unhappy?"

"No. All I'm saying is, you're happy with a place to sleep at night, a warm body curled up next to you, a hot meal, and your horse. Women ... sometimes they need more." *I need more.* "Remember my eighteenth birthday when you took me to dinner and bought me that fancy purse?"

"Damn thing cost me over two hundred bucks. Coach or some shit like that."

"I still carry that purse, but it wasn't the gift that mattered. It was that you paid attention. You saw me look at those magazines and earmark the stuff I liked. Pay attention to the women in your life, Cade."

He shuffled his feet in the dirt. "Got it. Coach purses and shit."

She waved a dismissive hand at him. "You're hopeless." He was a man, so he probably wouldn't get it unless she spelled it out. Women needed love. Lots of love. They needed validation too. Most of all they needed to know that the people in their lives would see them. Truly see them and love them anyway.

"I gotta go. I know you hate Tom, but he's a hard

worker, so try to be cordial. I know you like Wyatt, so try to be less cordial. Remember, I love you."

"You're such an asshole."

He tipped his hat and swung back into the saddle.

She went inside in search of breakfast.

Abby had kept her promise. The cupboards were stocked with everything from canned chili to peanut butter. The freezer was filled with meat and frozen waffles. To the average person, a place to sleep and food in their belly would have been enough, but Trinity wanted more. She wanted Wyatt.

She popped a waffle into the toaster and ate it on the way to the stables. She spent several hours straightening the tack and oiling the spare saddles. When her phone rang, her heart lurched. She was torn. She wanted it to be Wyatt, but she didn't. Hearing his voice was like putting a peanut butter cup just out of her reach.

It wasn't. On the other end of the line was Tom.

"How did you get my number?"

"Come on, darlin'. I'm in tight with your brother."

"What do you want?"

"I'm starving, and I left my lunch in the refrigerator. I called Cade and asked if he was coming this way, but he said no. Told me to call you. Said you wanted to take Sable for a ride. Would you mind bringing me my lunch?"

She knew he was telling the truth because he knew about her desire to ride Sable.

"Where are you at?"

"I've got the herd in the area outside the shelter. I think once it gets fenced off, it will be pasture five."

She considered his request. It wasn't as if it was unreasonable. If he left what he was doing, it would take him an hour to ride back and another to return to the cattle. She had nothing to do until the horses came back from the range.

"Okay, I'll be there in about an hour."

"Thanks, Trin."

She hated that he used her family's nickname for her, but she let it go.

When she got to the house, his lunch was in the refrigerator. At least he wasn't lying about that.

She packed up a few extra items like bottles of water and saddled Sable.

The ride was relaxing. Cade's spare horse was a sweetheart. Riding a well-behaved horse was like kicking back in a luxury car. She didn't require much. In fact, Sable almost seemed to know where they were going.

The herd moseying about was her first clue she was close. Her heart rate ticked up a few notches. Not the way it did when Wyatt was near but that feeling a person got when they were watching a horror flick, and the guy with the chainsaw stood behind the unsuspecting victim. Tom always put her on edge.

She moved around the cattle. The sky seemed to grow darker. The first drop of rain fell, hitting her like a bullet, right between the eyes. She looked up and cursed the universe. "Couldn't you wait another hour?"

The answer came with a crack of lightning and the boom of thunder. Like yesterday, the heavens opened up, and a deluge of rain poured down. She got a glimpse of Tom moving toward the shelter.

"Take cover," he yelled.

She wanted to scream to the gods. Life was so unfair. It was too soon to enter the last place Wyatt had made love to her. Too soon to relive the embarrassment of being caught, but what choice did she have? She gave Sable a nudge and galloped to the shelter. She pulled Tom's lunch from her pack and let Sable loose to find refuge.

The first dings of hail sounded on the roof as she dashed inside.

"What a mess." She shook the rain from her shoulders and looked up. "Wow." Tom's face looked like he'd been hit by a truck. "Piss someone off?" She thrust his lunch into his hands and stepped back.

"Your boyfriend rearranged my face, but I got a few in. Seems like I'm always fighting for you."

All she wanted to do was get out of there, but the noise grew louder, which meant the hail was growing bigger.

"Don't lie to yourself. You're not fighting on my behalf. You're fighting on yours."

"Why is that, Trin?" He took a step forward. She moved so her back was against the door. "Why do you share your goodies with everyone else and not me?" He grabbed his crotch. "I've got a lot to offer."

"Not interested."

"Yes, you are." He tossed the bag to the table and pinned her between his body and the door. "I've got what you want."

"That's your problem, Tom. You think you're a damn wizard and know what I need. Right now, I need you to step back."

"If I don't?" He ground himself against her. The hard rise of his arousal pressed on her hipbone. "You gonna tell your brother?"

Bile rose in her throat. This wasn't the time to be weak. Her fuse had burned through, and the gunpowder had ignited.

The man had to be a masochist since he continued to

torture himself over her. She moved her hand between their bodies and cupped his bulge. "I hear you like it rough." She gave it a squeeze.

He leaned in until his mouth was at her ear. "I'll give it to you any way you like it."

She made sure she had a good grip before she twisted. "The thing is, asshat, I don't want what you're offering. I'd rather superglue my vagina shut before I ever let you in." She twisted until she heard a pop. She was certain she'd fractured his junk. He let out a howl and stumbled back.

It wasn't smart to enter a storm unprotected, but it was her only choice. She took off out the door into hail the size of small apricots. Each one came at her like a fastball. On the edge of the property near the fence, she curled into a bush, head down, hugging her knees, and rode it out.

Ten minutes of it beating against her back felt like an hour. When the storm passed, she was afraid to look at the damage, afraid that she'd look like she'd been flogged.

With the last of her energy, she whistled, knowing Sable would come. When she did, she swung into the saddle, turned the horse in the right direction, and cried all the way home.

The hoofbeats behind her made her push Sable faster. When she got to the stable, Wyatt was on the porch.

Tom rode in a minute later with a smirk on his face. "You got to love that shelter. Cot's a little stiff, right, Trin?"

Wyatt looked at her with a question in his eyes.

"If you think that," she said, "you're as big an idiot as he is."

"She couldn't wait to get her hands on my junk," Tom bragged.

"That part is true. I grabbed his junk and twisted it so hard he should piss blood for the next week."

Wyatt winced. He turned to Tom and flipped him off before he stepped off the porch on his way to her. "Three, we need to talk."

She held up her hand. "Not now. I don't have it in me to say another word to anyone."

Painfully, she led Sable into the stable. It took all the strength she had left to pull off the saddle and give her the care she deserved. When she finished, she walked past the bunkhouse and Wyatt, and went straight to Abby's.

Everything hurt, including her heart. She raised her hand to knock, but Abby opened the door before she connected her knuckles to the wood.

"Oh, holy hell. You got caught in it." She pulled her inside. "Take off your wet shirt." Abby ran to her bedroom and came back with jars of cream, a dry shirt, and a pair of sweatpants. "Let me see."

Trinity winced when she pulled at her blouse. Thankfully it buttoned in front, so all she had to do was shrug it off, but the shrugging was hard. Each time she moved, the feel of a rusty blade dug into her back.

"Oh, honey. Why didn't you go to the shelter?" Abby dipped three fingers into a jar of gold-colored cream and applied it gently to Trinity's back.

"I did, but ..." She choked back a sob. She was always calm in the storm and waited until she was by herself to fall apart. Only this time she couldn't postpone her anguish. "The shelter posed a bigger threat than the storm."

"You need to tell Cade."

She shook her head. "That's not our way. I'm a Mosier. I own my shit." *Or I run from it.* She thought about Blain's offer. It looked more appealing each moment. "I handled it." She hoped to God she'd made Tom a eunuch.

"This is serious."

Trinity laughed. It was a defense mechanism when things got to be too much. "Seriously good stuff. What are you putting on my back?"

"Golden Salve. It's like magic bee cream." Abby finished applying the miracle salve and was helping her pull on the dry T-shirt when Cade walked in.

He stopped and stared. "What the hell happened? Tom said you sheltered under a tree with him?"

Trinity grabbed the sweatpants and gave Abby a hug. "Thanks for the help." She turned to Cade. "Yep, that's exactly what happened. He hovered over me and protected me because he's that kind of guy." She walked out and went straight to the trailer, where she locked the door and cried herself to sleep.

CHAPTER TWENTY-TWO

He'd sat in the living room all night to make sure Three got home safely. She never returned. He thought maybe she'd slept in the trailer, but the lights never went on. All of his text messages went unanswered.

His last hope was that she'd spent the night at Abby and Cade's.

Wyatt rose from the weathered chair in the corner and pushed past Tom, who limped into the room. No doubt Three had done a number on him like she'd said.

He shoved him into the wall on his way out of the bunkhouse.

"You're lucky I don't kill you. You don't touch what's mine and live. Out of respect for Trinity and her brother, I'm holding back."

Tom stood his ground, but his stoic expression gave way to fear as Wyatt passed. "If I were you, I'd be looking for another job."

"Don't forget your place. I've been here longer than you." Wyatt marched toward the cabin, trying to formulate his thoughts. This wasn't going to work out. Like

Three, his loyalties were being tested. A man couldn't be a servant to several masters. He really had to think about himself. At his age, things weren't getting easier; they were getting tougher. If he didn't watch himself, he'd be another Jimmy, throwing himself on the mercy of others. He didn't fault the old guy for displacing him. Maybe it was a blessing in disguise. Often the doors you're not supposed to walk through are closed, leading you closer to the door you are.

He had goals, and staying here working under Tom would never work. He had enough money saved to take care of him and Three for a while. They'd leave the ranch and find a place together.

His boots hit the stairs heavy. He marched across the porch and pounded on the door. It was early, but not too early for a rancher.

Cade flung open the door. His expression was anything but friendly.

"Wyatt. What can I do for you?"

"Can I come in?"

Cade stepped aside, and Wyatt entered.

"Just stopped by to tell you that I'm leaving. I'll give you two weeks to find someone else, but the sooner, the better."

His statement must have shocked Cade because he stumbled back.

Abby walked down the hallway. "Mornin', Wyatt. Would you like some coffee?"

He tipped his head. "Thank you for the offer, but this isn't a social call."

"I don't imagine it is, but you can have coffee just the same. Cream and sugar?"

"That would be fine." He wasn't picky; he took it any way it came.

"Have a seat. Let's talk about why you're leaving."

Cade led him to the kitchen table. He was afraid to sit in the spindly chairs. They looked too delicate for a man like him.

"They won't break. I promise you that. Abby says the chairs are over a hundred years old. They knew their stuff back then. They're probably glued together with the sap of the trees they cut down to build this house."

Wyatt sat and took the coffee from Abby. It was far too sweet for his tastes, but he drank it just the same. Maybe she could see the saltiness in his demeanor and thought he could use something sweet.

"I came down from Montana to work with Lloyd."

"Bozeman, right?"

He nodded. "Yep, I was at the Starling Ranch."

"Good outfit."

"It is but no room for growth. Their foreman has been there for years, and he's too stubborn to die, so I imagine he'll outlive the owners. Not that I'd wish death on the man. The point is, there's no room for advancement. I don't want to be a ranch hand the rest of my life. I want to be a foreman. When I answered Lloyd's call for help, he said he needed a right-hand man. I stepped up, thinking he wanted a foreman." He shook his head. "He had a son he never mentioned. I arrived and found out I'd fall under the super-vision of a kid who hadn't even busted his cherry much less run a ranch." He looked at Abby. "Sorry, ma'am."

"I've heard worse." She smiled. "Said worse."

Cade nodded. "Her worst is usually directed at me."

"Anyway," Wyatt continued, "I'm not a bag of sugar

that can be loaned out when someone needs to borrow some. I want a permanent position on a ranch that values my mind and my skillset. This isn't the ranch for me."

Cade cocked his head. "You don't like my ranch?"

He knew he had nothing to lose by saying what was on his mind. "The ranch is fine, and I'm sure you're a great guy, but honestly, I don't think you're looking at the big picture. You're growing too fast, and you're making decisions without thought." He held up his hand when Cade opened his mouth to defend himself. "You should be more selective about who works on your property."

"You're speaking of Tom?"

Abby grunted her disapproval. "Told you. I can see an asshole a mile away. Hell, I wouldn't be surprised if my bees up and left too. They're intuitive about danger."

"Tom isn't an asset. He's a liability. I haven't been able to talk to your sister since she got caught in the storm yesterday, but I know being pelted by hail was a better choice than staying in the shelter with him."

"Tom said they sheltered under a tree together."

"Well, who are you going to believe? Tom or your sister? It's not my objective to offend you, but honestly, you're a shit brother, and she deserves more." He rose, but Cade asked him to stay.

Wyatt turned to Abby. "Did Trinity sleep here? I'm worried about her."

Abby's expression turned serious. "No, I took care of her wounds, and she left. She didn't sleep in the bunkhouse?"

He shook his head. "No, and she's not answering her phone. I haven't beat the trailer door down, but there weren't any lights on last night, so I figured she stayed here."

Cade picked up his phone and dialed her. He waited several seconds. "No answer."

He called Tom next and asked him to come to the house.

Abby phoned Trinity. She shook her head like she couldn't get through, and then her eyes lit up. "Trinity, this is Abby. Can you come to the house?" She listened for a few minutes. "Yes, they are here, but this isn't for them, it's for me." She hung up. "She's on her way, but she doesn't want to talk to any of you. She's coming to talk to me."

That stung Wyatt. He was in love with her and was ready to pack up and go nomad to be with her.

He took his seat again and tapped his fingers on the table until he heard footsteps on the porch. They weren't heavy enough to be Tom's, so he knew they were Three's.

As soon as she walked inside, he moved straight to her. She held up her hand. He pulled her into his arms anyway until she screamed out in pain.

"What the hell?" He spun her around and lifted her shirt. She was black and blue. Every so often, there were small scrapes and abrasions that split her skin. "God, I'm going to kill him."

"I told you I took care of it."

"Baby, he's still walking, and that isn't good enough." He kissed her head and whispered, "I've given your brother my notice. We're leaving as soon as he finds my replacement."

She whirled around to face him. "We are?"

"Yep, there's only one thing for me here, and that's you," he whispered. "If I'm here, I can't have you. I refuse to work for Tom."

Abby took Three's arm and led her away. "Let's put

more cream on that back." They disappeared down the hallway.

A moment later, a knock sounded at the door.

Before Cade answered it, he turned to Wyatt. "Let me handle this. When I'm finished, you can beat the living shit out of him. When you're finished, I'll complete the job, or I'll start, and you end it."

As soon as he nodded, Cade opened the door. "Tom, come on in."

He eyed Wyatt and looked around as if searching for others.

"I don't know what he told you, but it's bullshit. He's so whipped it's unbelievable. You know your sister."

Cade fisted his hands. "I do know her, and I know she attracts a lot of attention because she's beautiful, but I also know she's smart and honest and loyal. She's also a badass." He waved Tom inside and closed the door behind him. "The boys used to pass rumors about her because everyone wanted her. My brother and father would beat the hell out of them. It got to the point where no one would go near her." He chuckled. "She made us promise not to defend her honor, that she'd deal with it herself. We gave her that because she was a Mosier. She was born to be tough. Raised to be tough. She is tough, but I forget that she's tough on the outside and soft in her heart. I respected her choice to take care of herself. But you know what? She told me a story yesterday. It was about Coach purses and paying attention. I realize that I haven't been truly looking in front of me. I see what I want to see. My sister is a storm. She can cause destruction, but she rarely hits dangerous levels unless it's warranted. Right now, she's a hurricane spinning at hundreds of miles per hour. I've been stupid to not watch while she gained speed."

Tom lifted his hand. "What the hell does this have to do with me?"

"Everything." Cade took a step forward while Tom took a step back. "All I saw when you both showed up was trouble. You two butted heads in Wyoming. I thought you were the blessing, and she was the curse. Not so. Turn around and show me your back."

"What the hell, man?"

Wyatt leaned against the door, making sure there was no escape for Tom.

"Do it!" Cade yelled.

He turned around and lifted his shirt to show smooth, tawny skin.

"You're a liar, Tom. You told me you sheltered under a tree with my sister." He turned to face the hallway. "Trin, I need you out here, sweetheart."

She must have been listening closely because she and Abby appeared in seconds.

"Show me your back."

Trinity didn't argue; she turned and lifted the T-shirt to reveal ugly black, blue, and purple bruises.

Cade moved so fast even Wyatt was stunned. He gripped Tom's collar and twisted it to choke the man. "You were in the shelter, and she chose to go outside because it was safer."

Tom pushed him away. "You're all crazy."

"Well, you're fired." He stepped back and looked at Wyatt. "I'm a man of my word. You can take him out and give him a beatdown or let him go. The choice is yours."

Three stepped forward. "No, the choice is mine." She

marched over to Tom and punched him in his already broken nose.

He cried like a baby. "Why is it always my damn nose?"

Three stepped back. "Because I already broke your dick." She pointed to the door. "Out."

"You want some tea?" Abby asked.

"Love some." She shook her hand and moved to the kitchen. "I need ice and more salve."

Cade watched Tom run for the door. When he left, he turned to Wyatt. "I've got a proposition for you." He pointed to the couch and chair where they took seats. "I can't pay you a ton, but I'll offer you the position of foreman of Mosier Ranch. Your incentive to stay is owning a percentage. Each year you'll continue to earn equity, up to thirty percent."

"You're offering me a percentage of profits or a percentage of the actual ranch?"

"The ranch, which comes with the profits. You take a day to think about it. We can come up with the details later, but I'm thinking an increase in your current wages, you still get to live in the bunkhouse, and you get a percentage of the assets. That way, you have an incentive to make the ranch profitable." He pointed to the door. "I need to talk to my sister, and you've got shit to do."

Wyatt looked at Three, who was smiling despite her pain. "Can we talk later?"

She sighed. "How about tomorrow? I'm really beat. I just want to sleep for a week."

His heart sank to his boots. He needed her now, but this was her choice, and he'd respect it. "Tomorrow then."

CHAPTER TWENTY-THREE

Trinity carried her tea to the table and took a seat. Everything hurt, from her back to her knuckles to her heart. Earlier, Wyatt had told her they were going to leave together. That was before Cade offered him everything. She knew he'd never get another deal like that anywhere. Ownership of a ranch was beyond his dreams, and she'd never take that away from him.

She wouldn't beg her brother to change his stance of mixing money and love. If it didn't work out between them, one would have to leave, and she knew he'd offer, but she'd never allow it. She had options. Blain wanted her back. She was in a position to negotiate. When she had gone to work for him before, she was desperate to have someplace to belong. She was in the same position, but he didn't know it.

"Trinity, I owe you an apology. I tough loved you in hopes that you'd figure your way out," Cade said.

Abby cleared her throat. "Really? You're going to use the tough love excuse for your behavior?" She turned and walked toward the hallway. "I'll start packing your shit."

She glanced back at Trinity. "Do you spoon? I ask because I like to be big spoon. It's the only time I can be big anything."

Cade growled. "No one's packing anything." He looked back to Trinity. "I'm a fricking idiot. Obsessed with advancing the ranch, I overlooked what was important. You are. Sometimes I lose sight of my priorities, and it takes someone or something to make me rethink my positions. I've always known you weren't sleeping around. Dad would have locked you up. I also know that I shouldn't have listened when you said you could handle it. You shouldn't have had to." He looked at Abby.

"You're getting there. Keep going."

"I love you, Trin. You're my family. You belong here with me. Abby has offered the spare bedroom. You should take it. It's yours."

Abby smiled and walked away.

The problem was she didn't want the spare bedroom. She wanted Wyatt. Him offering her the spare room meant that he hadn't changed his position on her having a relationship with someone working at the ranch. That was the general rule everywhere. Workplace romances were frowned upon. She understood and couldn't argue. Look at what their relationship had done so far. Tom had been fired, and Wyatt was the only one left.

She knew if she went back to the bunkhouse and told him she wanted to leave, he would take her away. He'd give up everything he wanted just to please her. But because she loved him, she was willing to give him up so he could have his dream.

"I should get going. I've got a lot to do." She gave him a weak smile. "The horses don't shovel their shit or feed themselves."

"I'll take care of it," he said. "You've got to be hurting."

"Well, I feel like a bull knocked me on my ass and trampled over me, but I know it will feel worse if I don't move."

"Has anyone ever told you how stubborn you are?"

"You have countless times." She walked to him and lifted on her tiptoes to kiss his cheek. "Thanks for everything."

"See you later?"

She nodded. "Yep, definitely later."

She slogged her way to the stables. Tom had already loaded Willow and left. She felt bad for the sweet mare. Deep down, she hoped that Willow would reach the end of her fuse soon and turn around and bite Tom or buck him off.

She took care of Sable and Red.

"Seems like I'm always saying goodbye," she said as she nuzzled into Red's muzzle. "You be a good boy." She walked over to Sable and gave her some loving too. These horses would be fine. They were treasured and cared for. Hell, most good cowboys took better care of their horses than they did themselves.

It hurt her heart to think about leaving everyone. Most of her family was in Aspen Cove. She knew, with a little prodding, they would have been able to get her father there too.

On a final attempt to give herself a reason to stay, she leaned against Sable's stall and dialed Goldie. If she thought Jake Powers would be gone within the week, she'd rough it out here and move into the rustic cabin when he left. That was a win-win. Surely, she could find a job doing something else. Something she hated but would put up with for a chance to properly date Wyatt. Cade couldn't say much if she wasn't living or working on the ranch.

Goldie picked up on the third ring. "Hello, girlfriend."

Trinity swallowed the lump of sorrow. She'd never had girlfriends. Most women didn't understand her because she was a cowgirl, and those that did didn't like her because their men did.

"When did you say Jake Powers was leaving?"

"He just got here. He's got the big reveal, and then he said something about getting someone to run whatever it is he's revealing." She laughed. "This is worse than wondering what's behind curtain number one on Let's Make a Deal."

"It's always a donkey in a hat," Trinity said.

"Lord, I hope not. With those construction crews fixing up the old houses in the area, we have enough asses here. What we need are more good men."

"Are you getting ready to trade Tilden in?"

"No way, just thinking about the singles in town like Natalie, who should be back soon. Then there's Mercy Meyer, the schoolteacher from Copper Creek. Deanna, who is Samantha's assistant. She's been talking about moving here too. We've got that artist Sosie Grant, but she hasn't been here for a while. There's also Brenda, who is Deanna's assistant. Wouldn't it be nice to have an assistant who had an assistant? With that property development guy Mason Van Der Veen buying up all those houses and refurbishing them, there's bound to be more people coming in. I just hope they're as nice as you."

"You should start a local gossip column and post it with your vlog."

Goldie laughed. "Not on your life. First off, I'm dyslexic, so letters aren't really my thing, but printed gossip gets you in trouble. When I talk on the phone, I have deniability."

"I knew you were smart."

"Anyway, I'll let you know when the place opens up. I'd say at the earliest a month, the latest maybe two or three."

She tried not to let her disappointment show in her voice. This was a sign that the universe wanted her to move on. "Sounds great. I've got to go. Work to do and all that."

"Talk to you soon," Goldie said.

"Yep, soon." She wouldn't talk to Goldie anytime in the near future. Goodbyes were too hard.

She made her way into the bunkhouse. She had a lot more than she came with. More than her backpack could handle. This time she'd be smarter. No way was she leaving her underwear behind. She didn't want anyone to know because they'd give a hundred reasons to stay. The reason to leave was bigger and more important—Wyatt. She wanted him to have everything, and at Mosier Ranch, he could. Well, everything but her. Someday he'd find a woman who wouldn't be a conflict of interest. Maybe it would be one of those women Goldie mentioned. The waitress or the artist or the assistant or assistant's assistant would have enough separation from the ranch to be perfect.

The tightness in her chest almost hurt as much as the bruises on her back. She took the paper sack the donated clothes had come in and filled it up. Making sure no one was around to see, she snuck it to her SUV. She made two trips, the last including the pictures on her dresser. She stared at the woman who had birthed her. Maybe she'd done the same thing. Maybe her leaving had allowed her father and brothers to have the life they wanted. She'd always considered her mother to be selfless, but maybe she was being selfless. Often, the truth looked different from someone else's perspective. Sadly, only her mother knew.

Just before it was time for Wyatt to come in from the range, she locked her bedroom door and closed it. To leave it open would show her hand. She knew Wyatt would respect her wishes and leave her alone, especially if the door was locked. They'd figure out how to unlock it later. She took a few things from the cupboards and walked to the trailer.

This was where her journey began, and where it would end.

She opened the can of stew and a fresh package of crackers. While it heated, she texted Blain.

I'll be there tomorrow night. I want my bungalow back. Make sure it's clean and fully stocked with food. I also want Pride to be my horse. I'll expect a ten percent raise on top of everything. And the next time I leave, it will be because I want to not because you're throwing me out. If you can't agree to all my demands, I'll stay where I'm at.

She pressed send and held her breath. If he didn't come back with a yes, then she had no idea what she'd do. It was all a bluff.

His text pinged.

See you tomorrow. Angel is excited.

She laughed.

One more thing. Don't lie.

Another message came in.

Okay, she's in tears, but she'll survive.

She dished up a bowl of stew and crumbled crackers on top. She sat at the tiny table and took a breath. Everything was set. She knew Texas wasn't a long-term plan. No way would she torture Angel to sit in the saddle when she wanted to be somewhere else—she deserved choices too—but that was a fight for another day.

CHAPTER TWENTY-FOUR

Wyatt decided to wait Three out. He knew she'd be up to feed the horses and clean out the stalls. That's why he woke up early. He wasn't letting another day go by where they didn't talk it out. He missed her. Missed everything about her. She was so much more than a spark to his day. She was the sun.

He made the coffee and cooked up a big breakfast of bacon and toast and eggs.

"Three, breakfast is ready," he called out.

There wasn't a hint of life in the house. No groan when her feet hit the cold floor. No movement of air. No scent of her shampoo or body wash.

He moved down the hall to her door and knocked softly. Pressing his ear to the wood, he listened but heard nothing. The second knock was louder.

"Trin, get up, and have breakfast with me."

Again, there wasn't a peep from the other side. He turned the door handle to find it locked. No way had she slept through everything. He pounded once more.

"Damn it, Trinity, get your ass out here. I need you."

The truth of that statement twisted his heart. She was his today, his tomorrow, and all the days to come.

When silence greeted him once more, fear seeped into his pores. She'd been hurt in the storm. What if she was lying in the bed unable to move? What if she'd fallen asleep to never wake up again?

He shouldered the door open, breaking the lock in the process. He stared at the empty bed, the closet, where hangers swayed in the breeze. The pictures of her family nowhere in sight. He wasn't prepared for his next question. What if she'd left?

He rushed outside to find her SUV gone. He turned and ran to the main house to get Cade. His knock wasn't the soft gentle rap of someone who feared they'd wake everyone. It was intended to stir the dead.

Cade swung open the door with fire in his eyes. "What the hell is wrong? There better be someone bleeding or a fire."

"We need to go after your sister."

Cade looked at him like he was speaking in tongues. "What do you mean?" He wiped the sleep from his eyes.

"She's gone. Packed up her shit and left."

Abby walked out, tugging a sweatshirt over her T-shirt. "Trinity is gone?" She moved straight to the kitchen to put on a pot of coffee.

"Maybe she went into town to get muffins or something."

"No way. She left," Wyatt said. "I'm going after her."

"Wait." Cade rushed barefooted down the hallway.

While he was gone, Abby poured three cups of coffee and made six slices of toast.

"I refuse to live without her. If that means I have to leave the ranch, then I will," Wyatt said.

Abby pushed a mug of coffee into his hand. "Why would you have to live without her? Cade told her to stay. He offered you the promotion." She shook her head and went about buttering toast.

Cade walked into the kitchen, shaking his head. "She left because I offered her the spare bedroom."

Abby rolled her eyes. "Of course you did. You're her brother, and you love her."

Cade picked up a cup of coffee and downed it.

Wyatt didn't know how the heat hadn't seared Cade's tonsils.

"I know her, and what she heard was, *you can stay, but you can't stay with Wyatt.*"

Abby spun around and fisted her hips. "That's not what you meant." She stared at Cade with the intensity of a hawk eyeing a mouse.

"Well..." Cade muttered.

Abby shoved two slices of toast into each of his hands. She marched past Cade and pulled her keys from the hook by the door. "If I didn't love you so much, I swear I'd kill you. Let's go. We have to find her."

They all rushed from the door and climbed into Abby's truck.

It struck Wyatt funny that Cade sat in the middle while the tiny woman drove.

She reached over and slugged Cade in the thigh. "Why in the hell are you allowed to be in love on your ranch, and your sister isn't? Don't you understand how hard it is to find the one?" She started the engine and tore down the gravel road, kicking up dust behind her. "I'm thinking maybe you're not the one for me if you can overlook love so easily."

Cade hung his head. "Would it help if I told you I'm blinded by my love for you?"

Wyatt choked on his coffee.

"Yes, it will. At least you know what love looks like. It's not always pretty." She turned onto the paved road toward town. "I remember a man willing to kill a bear for me. I saw the fear in your eyes when you thought you'd lost me. How do you think Wyatt feels?"

Cade turned to look at him. "I'm so sorry, man. I didn't know it was at that place."

Wyatt searched the road for any sign of Three's white SUV. "You know I can't take the job as your foreman if Trinity can't be by my side."

Cade was silent until Abby elbowed him. "Fine. I don't care who you love or what you do. Just don't wreck the ranch."

"Where would she go?" Wyatt asked.

They drove through town hoping to find her, but at five in the morning, the streets were empty.

"We've got two choices," Abby said. "We go north or south. She's either heading to places unknown or back to where she came from."

"Go south," Wyatt said. "She had a good relationship with an old man they called Trigger at Wallaby Ranch."

"We're driving to Texas?" Cade asked. "What about—"

"Really?" Abby yelled.

Cade changed his tune. "We're driving to Texas and let me tell you, my sister is worth the trip."

Wyatt wasn't sure he meant that or if he was giving Abby what she wanted to hear, but it was the truth. Three was worth any distance they'd have to travel to get her back.

For a tiny thing, Abby had a lead foot. Cade kept telling her to slow down while he told her to speed up. He'd be happy to pay any ticket she got. They made it two hours south when he saw her SUV pulled into a gas station.

His heart took off like a wild stallion. When Abby pulled into the station, Wyatt jumped out.

Trinity wasn't anywhere in sight.

"Don't wait for me. If I'm back in a few hours, it means we're staying, and if I'm not, she didn't want to return. I'm going where Three is going."

"Are you sure you don't want us to wait?" Abby asked.

"No, I need to do this alone. I need to convince her that I'm worth the fight."

"She won't come back if she thinks she's not welcome." Cade rummaged around Abby's glove compartment until he found a pen and a piece of paper. He wrote something on the back of Abby's proof of insurance and handed it to Wyatt. "Give her this."

He shoved it in his pocket and marched into the station. He found her looking at the candy bars, reaching for a package of Reese's cups.

"I hear you'd do just about anything for peanut butter and chocolate."

Her hand stilled. She didn't turn to look at him. "What are you doing here?"

"It's a long story. Grab your stuff, and I'll tell you outside."

She swiped the candy from the rack and turned to face him.

His heart nearly broke at the sight of her. Despite the dark circles below her eyes and the red rims caused by hours of tears, she was stunning.

"You left me." The words came out choked.

"I left you so you could have your dream."

"I've got nothing if I don't have you." He felt the tears pooling behind his eyelids. "Do you really need that candy?"

She nodded.

He walked her to the register and searched his pocket for his wallet, but he'd forgotten everything at the ranch. "I'd pay, but I left without anything."

"What happened to my boy scout?" She paid for the candy and her gas and walked outside with him.

The sun was rising and cast a glow over the mountain, washing everything in its path with light and hope.

"I can't live without my heart. You took it with you when you drove away."

She moved to the picnic bench that sat on a patch of grass to the side of the gas station.

"Wyatt, everything you want is back in Aspen Cove."

They took a seat, straddling the bench and staring at one another.

He shook his head. "Not everything. I want you more than I want anything else."

"You're willing to give it all up for me?" Her eyes narrowed.

"Three, you're it. Without you, nothing matters. Don't you get it?"

She cocked her head to the side. "I get that you love me. I love you, and that's why I left. When you truly love someone, you put them first."

"You're right, and it's why I told your brother I might not return. I'm a leaf caught in your wind. Wherever you blow, I'll follow."

"You can't mean that."

He pulled her forward, so they were knee to knee. "Trinity Mosier, my fate is in your hands. We have two choices. We get in that SUV and drive to wherever you were headed together, or we turn around and go home."

"I was going back to Texas."

"You hated that job."

"True, but I like to eat. He texted yesterday and asked me to come back."

"Ah, Three, he doesn't deserve you." He knew he had to be careful and not push too hard. He wanted her to choose him, not feel like he was the lesser of two evils.

"I renegotiated my employment contract. I don't expect it to be a forever plan but a stop-gap until I can find something better."

A fist in his chest squeezed his heart so painfully he gasped. When he took his next breath, he exhaled the words, "I'm better, Three. I know you. I see you. I love you. I'd get on my knees and beg you to come home with me, but I don't want to choose for you. You choose for me. I'm all in whether it's Texas, Colorado, or someplace else."

"I'm not choosing for you. That's so unfair. I know what it's like to have others decide."

"I know, sweetheart, but this time the choice is yours. The only way I can get what I want is to follow you. Where are we going, Three?"

She chewed her lip. "I just want what's best for you. Wyatt, Mosier Ranch is where you should be, but I can't be there and not have you."

He remembered the note Cade handed him. He'd shoved it in the front pocket of his jeans when he entered the station. "This is from your brother." He prayed it said something kind because if it didn't, his first move would be back to Mosier Ranch to kick the man's ass.

She opened it. "Abby's insurance policy?"

Wyatt lifted his shoulders. "We had to do things on the fly. He wrote something on the back."

She turned it over and read. Her eyes sparkled with unshed tears. She swiped at the first one to fall. "He wrote this?"

She turned the note toward him.

Come home, Trinity. Not to my house with Abby but your place with Wyatt.

Love your hardheaded brother, Cade

"Yes, and he even rode in the center seat of her truck all the way here."

She laughed. "No way."

"Seriously. That woman has your brother's heart all twisted up inside, but she didn't tell him what to write. That came from him."

She stared at the page for a moment and then lifted her eyes to his. "What about Blain Wallaby and his daughter Angel?"

"He'll have to find his own Trinity. You're mine today, tomorrow, and always."

"And you want me to go back to Aspen Cove with you?"

"More than I want my next breath." He leaned in and pressed his forehead to hers. "I want to spend all my time with you, not missing you. Let's go home. We'll take the day off and spend it in bed practicing for the day you tell me you want to have my baby."

Her eyes grew wide. "You want a baby with me?"

"Sweetheart, I want to experience life with you, and

that comes with babies and wrinkles and gray hair and arthritis."

She laughed. "You had me at baby, but when you added wrinkles and gray hair ... how could a woman say no to that?"

He kissed her and held her tightly to him, afraid if he let go, she'd disappear. Moments later, when he released her, he stood and walked with her to the SUV.

"Are you going to call Blain and tell him you got a different deal?"

She tossed him her keys and climbed into the passenger side. "Nope, but I'll text him. That's how he offered me my job back. Seems fair that it's the way I'll give him a two-minute notice."

He started the engine. "Are you sure you trust me to drive? I don't have my driver's license on me."

"I'm trusting you with my future and my heart. Surely I can trust you to get me home."

"Home it is." He chuckled. "You know what's funny?"

"I'm sure you're going to tell me."

"I'm finally going to be a foreman, and I have no one to boss around."

She unbuckled and slid into the seat next to him. "Sure you do. You're the boss of my heart."

CHAPTER TWENTY-FIVE

She snuck out of bed early and turned the alarm off before it could wake Wyatt. They'd been home for a week now, and every day was better than the last. What started as a stopover until she could make her next move became her ending point and forever. Who would have thought that being fired, rejected, and beaten by a hailstorm could turn out so amazing, but if her life with Wyatt was anything like the preview she'd lived last week, she wanted to spend a lifetime at Mosier Ranch in his arms.

She made the coffee and snuck out the front door to the stables. Each time she stepped inside, she didn't see the work ahead. Sure, there were stalls to muck, horses to feed, and tack to clean, but what she saw was love. Love of a man who gave her his horse.

"Hey, handsome." She walked to Red's stall and smiled. She had two men in her life. One she rode during the day and one who rode her at night.

She saddled him and took off toward the pasture where her brother had moved the cattle yesterday. She figured she'd get started early while Wyatt got a little more sleep.

"Three," she heard him yell from the porch. She turned Red around and headed home.

"Don't be yelling. You'll wake the valley," she said.

"I woke up, and you weren't there."

She swung down from her horse and tied his lead to the porch. She wished Red came with a whistle like her brother's horses, but he didn't. If given enough leeway, he would take off for the hills. It wasn't that he didn't like living on the ranch, but he was a horse, and horses liked the wind in their hair.

"I was trying to surprise you and start moving the herd."

He smiled. "You were?"

He hopped down from the porch and swept her into his arms. "How about we go back to bed, and I'll surprise you? You know that thing I do with my lips and your—"

She covered his mouth with her hand. "Yes, I know exactly what you're talking about, but my brother and Abby don't need to know."

He laughed as he took long strides up the stairs and into the house. "They have to know by now. You're a passionate, receptive lover, and I'm sure they've heard your *More Wyatt* multiple times." He strode down the hall to his bedroom, where they'd traded the twin beds for a queen. He tossed her on the mattress. "In fact, I think your brother is sending the Coopers out to see if there's a way to insulate the bunkhouse."

She opened her mouth. "No. He did not say that to you."

Wyatt tugged off her boots and pulled down her

jeans. "No, but I like it when you turn pink with embarrassment. You're so damn cute."

She lifted up on her elbows and watched him drop his jeans and work his way from her ankles to that sensitive spot on the inside of her knee.

"Shouldn't we be in the field?"

"You're exactly where you should be, and that's nearly naked in my bed."

"What about the cows?"

He nibbled on the inside of her thigh.

"Cows have been taking care of themselves for centuries. They can wait another hour or so."

"An hour?"

"At least." He pressed his lips against her core. After several sensuous strokes, he said, "All work and no play makes Wyatt a dull boy."

She lay back and took in the love he gave. The first climax came quickly. He knew her body like it was his own. Then again, she'd given herself to him completely the day they returned to the ranch.

She was primed to let go again when he moved between her legs.

"I love you more than anything, Three."

She stared into his eyes. Eyes that held the answers to all her questions but one.

"Why do you love me?"

He pressed inside her body. "Because my heart didn't give me a choice."

Up next is One Hundred Decisions

Wilde Love Series

Betting On Him

Betting On Her

Betting On Us

A Wilde Love Collection

The Boys of Fury Series

Redeeming Ryker

Saving Silas

Delivering Decker

The Boys of Fury Boxset

Making the Grade Series

The Dean's List

Honor Roll

The Learning Curve

Making the Grade Box Set

Stand Alone Billionaire Novels

Dream Maker

JOIN MY READER'S CLUB AND GET A FREE BOOK.

Go to www.authorkellycollins.com

ABOUT THE AUTHOR

International bestselling author of more than thirty novels, Kelly Collins writes with the intention of keeping love alive. Always a romantic, she blends real-life events with her vivid imagination to create characters and stories that lovers of contemporary romance, new adult, and romantic suspense will return to again and again.

For More Information
www.authorkellycollins.com
kelly@authorkellycollins.com

Printed in Great Britain
by Amazon

37490381R00126